# SECRETS

## Lindsay McKenna

**Blue Turtle Publishing**

# Praise for Lindsay McKenna

"A treasure of a book... highly recommended reading that everyone will enjoy and learn from."

—Chief Michael Jaco, US Navy SEAL, retired, on Breaking Point

"Readers will root for this complex heroine, scarred both inside and out, and hope she finds peace with her steadfast and loving hero. Rife with realistic conflict and spiced with danger, this is a worthy page-turner."

—BookPage.com on Taking Fire
March 2015 Top Pick in Romance

"... is fast-paced romantic suspense that renders a beautiful love story, start to finish. McKenna's writing is flawless, and her story line fully absorbing. More, please."

—Annalisa Pesek, Library Journal on Taking Fire

"Ms. McKenna masterfully blends the two different paces to convey a beautiful saga about love, trust, patience and having faith in each other."

—Fresh Fiction on Never Surrender

"Genuine and moving, this romantic story set in the complex world of military ops grabs at the heart."

—RT Book Reviews on Risk Taker

"McKenna does a beautiful job of illustrating difficult topics through the development of well-formed, sympathetic characters."

—Publisher's Weekly (starred review) on Wolf Haven
One of the Best Books of 2014, Publisher's Weekly

"McKenna delivers a story that is raw and heartfelt. The relationship between Kell and Leah is both passionate and tender. Kell is the hero every woman wants, and McKenna employs skill and s empathy to craft a physically and emotionally abused character in Leah. Using tension and steady pacing, McKenna is adept at expressing growing, tender love in the midst of high stakes danger."

—RT Book Reviews on Taking Fire

"Her military background lends authenticity to this outstanding tale, and readers will fall in love with the upstanding hero and his fierce determination to save the woman he loves.

—Publishers Weekly (starred review) on Never Surrender
One of the Best Books of 2014, Publisher's Weekly

"Readers will find this addition to the Shadow Warriors series full of intensity and action-packed romance. There is great chemistry between the characters and tremendous realism, making Breaking Point a great read."

—RT Book Reviews

"This sequel to Risk Taker is an action-packed, compelling story, and the sizzling chemistry between Ethan and Sarah makes this a good read."

—RT Book Reviews on Degree of Risk

"McKenna elicits tears, laughter, fist-pumping triumph, and most all, a desire for the next tale in this powerful series."

—Publishers Weekly (starred review) on Running Fire

"McKenna's military experience shines through in this moving tale . . . McKenna (High Country Rebel) skillfully takes readers on an emotional journey into modern warfare and two people's hearts."

—Publisher's Weekly on Down Range

"Lindsay McKenna has proven that she knows what she's doing when it comes to these military action/romance books."

—Terry Lynn, Amazon on Zone of Fire.

"At no time do you want to put your book down and come back to it later! Last Chance is a well written, fast paced, short (remember that) story that will please any military romance reader!"

—LBDDiaries, Amazon on Last Chance.

# Also available from
# Lindsay McKenna

## Blue Turtle Publishing

### DELOS

# Harlequin/HQN/Harlequin
# Romantic Suspense

## SHADOW WARRIORS
Danger Close
Down Range
Risk Taker
Degree of Risk
Breaking Point
Never Surrender
Zone of Fire
Taking Fire
On Fire
Running Fire

## THE WYOMING SERIES
Shadows From The Past
Deadly Identity
Deadly Silence
The Last Cowboy
The Wrangler
The Defender
The Loner
High Country Rebel
Wolf Haven
Night Hawk
Out Rider

## WIND RIVER VALLEY SERIES, Kensington

*2016*
Wind River Wrangler

*2017*
Wind River Rancher
Wind River Cowboy
Wind River Wrangler's Challenge

www.lindsaymckenna.com

Dear Reader,

SECRETS? We all have them, don't we? Yep. And maybe there are some we know about (those nasty skeletons in the closet that involve another family member, near or distant to you), and some we don't know about. Either way, secrets can either build us up once we know about them, or destroy us.

This is a novella sequel to Unbound Pursuit, 2B1. If you read Tangled Pursuit, Book 2, you were introduced to USMC Captain Tal Culver and US Navy SEAL Chief, Wyatt Lockwood. Their sequel was Unbound Pursuit.

A funny thing happened while I was writing about "what else" was happening in Tal and Wyatt's life. A secondary set of characters became very important to me and needed to have their story told, too. This involves Wyatt's younger sister, Mattie Lockwood, and the man in her life, Mark Reuss, who was a US Marine Corps recon for ten years, and a man who held terrible secrets, most of them bad. They were a fascinating couple. Mattie was the idealist; the person who always held hope in her heart for the most hopeless of people or situations. Mark, on the other hand, was the diametric opposite. He knew what reality looked like and that bred pessimism in him. He'd lost hope as a child.

Not only did Mark have secrets? The townspeople believed him to be a dark cloud that if he came into their lives, always muddied it up and made it worse, not better. Mark grew up believing that about himself because it had started with his alcoholic father, a Texas rancher.

Only Mattie saw his goodness and never gave up hope—or her love—for him.

This is their story. Please let me know how you enjoyed it. Catch me at www.lindsaymckenna.com.

Thank you for purchasing this book. I truly hope you enjoy it. If it leaves you with warm fuzzies, please think about writing a review on it for me. Reviews are VERY important and helpful in bringing new readers to my series. If you would love to review but never have, just get a hold of me at docbones224@earthlink.net and I'll send you my little article on how to write a dynamite review! Thank you!

# Dedication

I dedicate this book to all of my wonderful, die-hard readers! What would I do without you in my life? Thank you for loving the stories I write.

# CHAPTER 1

*December 23*

MARK REUSS WAS in such deep shit he couldn't see daylight anymore. His lower, left arm ached so badly he wanted to yell like a banshee, but the blackness of the Texas night, the biting December cold seeping into his body, made him call on all his Recon Marine skills to escape up the hill.

He kept his night-vision goggles over his eyes as he climbed. Below him ATF, DEA, Border Patrol, and FBI agents swarmed around several eighteen-wheeler trucks. Thanks to Mark, they'd made a surprise raid on Mexican drug lord Diego Cardona's vehicles, and now American agents were rounding up what was left of the members of his drug and sex-slave cartel.

Sixty kidnapped children from South and Central America, had been on their way across the border in the massive trucks, all part of Cardona's sex-trafficking operation that regularly took kidnapped children across Texas soil and on to the East Coast. Recently, the cartel had expanded from sex trading to running a monthly gun-and-run operation, as well. Because of Mark, who had been sent into the cartel as an undercover agent, US authorities had caught the transport, and this fortunate group of children had been saved.

Mark winced as he held his broken arm tightly against his Kevlar vest. Damn, it hurt! But it was worth it, he told himself, and he'd do it again to save those kids and dismantle the operation.

Below him, he'd just left his best friend, Wyatt Lockwood, who had been shot by one of Cardona's drug soldiers. The bullet had struck Lockwood's Kevlar vest and had lifted the ex-SEAL off his feet, slamming him backward into the slope. Mark had seen it happen from his Jeep, which had overturned during the melee, breaking his arm in the process. But all he had focused on was Wyatt, who lay dazed, out of breath, and fighting for his life. Skidding in front of Wyatt, Mark had turned, and shot and killed the drug soldier who'd been climbing up out of the ravine to finish Wyatt off.

Then, turning back to Wyatt, Mark had seen that his childhood friend lay gasping, his gloved hand pressed against his heart beneath his dented

Kevlar vest. The bullet had struck hard against it, causing his heart to lose its life-giving rhythm. He didn't know why Wyatt was out here, except that this had happened on his family's ranch. The last he'd heard, he had left the Navy, and was probably visiting his family over the Christmas holiday. Quickly, Mark told Wyatt to move his hand, closed his fist, and thumped the hell out of him. That thump had reset Wyatt's heart rhythm back to normal. Thank God he'd been able to save Wyatt's life tonight. Another win for the good guys! And a rare win for those poor, frightened children who'd been saved from a life worse than hell itself.

Mark moved silently up and over a hill covered with dried, dead grass. Prickly pear bushes and cholla cacti were strewn everywhere in the Guadalupe Mountains, especially on the lower slopes where the US agencies had lain in wait to attack Cardona's unsuspecting drivers.

Previously, Mark had gotten word to his DEA handler that the drug lord was going to use Rocking L Ranch as a back door to sneak into the US. And it just so happened that Wyatt's family lived on the ranch. Cardona had chosen it as a crossing point to avoid the Border Patrol from finding them at other known drug-running entry points.

Mark knew his intel had made this attack possible, and a thread of pleasure thrummed through him as he melted into the darkness on the other side of the hill. All the noise from the attack dissolved behind him as he began to trot down the slope, avoiding the cacti and thick brush.

He needed medical help. Mark knew at least one of the two bones in his lower arm was either cracked or broken. Pain drifted up his arm, into his shoulder, and he clenched his teeth now and then as the pain turned up in volume. He didn't dare walk into the Van Horn, Texas hospital because everyone would recognize him there; and there was no doc-in-a-box in that tiny Texas town, either.

His thoughts turned to his sister, Sage, who now ran the Diamond R Ranch near Van Horn. He could try to get to Sage, but then he'd have to explain that he was an undercover DEA agent, not a truck driver who drove goods between El Paso and Ciudad Juarez, Mexico and back, as everyone, including her, thought. He couldn't blow his cover.

If he went back to the family ranch for medical help, Sage would hammer him with questions as she helped set his arm. Sage was smart and sassy, and she would eventually force the intel out of him. No, he definitely could not go home to her! He couldn't tell her anything or his cover would be revealed, and his baby sister would not understand any of his reasons for doing such dark, dangerous work. He'd gone undercover, wore a beard, and changed his name, and Cardona did not know this was his home turf, or that the people belonging to these two ranches were his family and friends. If Cardona ever found out, he'd murder all of them, and there was no way Mark would put any of them in harm's way.

Besides, the other reason he couldn't go back to his family's ranch was because his abusive father, Jeb, still lived there in a smaller house on ranch property. Jeb was now wheelchair bound after a stroke five years ago, but Mark still hated him for his cruelty when they'd been children. He'd sworn years ago never to return to the family ranch as long as that bastard was still alive and living on the property.

Mark didn't know how Sage could tolerate the alcoholic. He had made their lives a living hell for eighteen years. But his little sister was tougher than he was emotionally. He knew Sage literally ignored Jeb and had hired a full-time male caregiver for him. He respected her set of balls. He couldn't have accomplished what she had: turn the failing ranch around after Jeb's stroke, and create a thriving, economically sound cattle company once again.

Mark adored Sage. He'd protected her from Jeb when they were growing up, and had taken the beatings meant for her from his father's fists and that thick leather belt he wore around his waist. The beltings he'd endured had caused deep bruising that had lasted for weeks afterward. Mark never regretted taking Sage's beatings. It was damn wrong for a father to beat his daughter—or his son, for that matter.

He continued to jog down the slight slope, dodging the thick groups of cacti and heading toward the road the government officials and law enforcement had driven in on an hour earlier. He wished he had a sling to hold his arm quiet against his body, but he didn't. The pain kept him alert as he moved swiftly through the night. Droplets of frozen moisture shot out of his mouth. He could barely see the headlight glow of all those vehicles on the other side of the Guadalupe Mountains now. Tonight, Cardona had lost all the children he was going to sell to sexual predators along the East Coast and his whole operation had gone bust. Triumph soared through him.

Mark made his way to the uneven dirt road that led back to a highway that would take him into Van Horn. He decided to go see Mattie Lockwood, Wyatt's younger sister, who lived on the edge of town. It was one a.m. and he knew she'd be fast asleep in her bed. Mark knew it would tear Mattie up to suddenly see him once again because they'd been best friends as children. Later, puppy love had blossomed between them when they were freshmen in high school. They'd had such dreams when they graduated— dreams that had later been destroyed.

But perhaps there was still something between them. He knew how loyal Mattie was, and he truly hoped she'd help him. She had a soft heart for everything and everyone. She wouldn't needle him relentlessly like Sage would. The last time he'd seen Mattie was four months ago when he'd lied and told her he was taking a job as a truck driver in El Paso that would have him living across the border, in Ciudad Juarez most of the time. Everyone in Van Horn knew he'd left town once again.

When he'd told her, her expression had gone blank, her freckled skin tightening across her cheeks as those incredibly large, beautiful green eyes went dark with hurt. They always carried a light that danced within them, but not after he told her that. Mark knew he'd hurt Mattie, and he hated it. He had loved her forever.

But dammit, life always interrupted them, and he could never tell her he loved her as much as he knew she loved him. He'd been born into bad luck and it had never gone away. Nothing he'd really wanted had ever manifested and all he'd brought to the people he loved was pain and heartache.

It was the most agonizing of all the decisions he'd ever made, leaving Van Horn again after being home from the Marine Corps only nine months ago. He'd thought he was home for good, but then he was summoned to go undercover by the DEA. He accepted the job, but every day, he regretted breaking the trust of loved ones. And yet, it had to be done.

He and Mattie had had such dreams—they'd get married after graduating high school, and he'd work on his father's ranch while she got her degree to teach kindergarten in Van Horn, ten miles from the Diamond R ranch. She loved children more than life, almost as much as she loved him. But all he'd ever done was to bring Mattie disappointment.

And now, he risked disappointing her again because he was going to ask her to help him, and then he'd have to leave her. Again. She wouldn't ask the questions Sage would because she wasn't a type A personality like his sister. Fortunately, she was an easygoing, laid back Type B, a safe harbor for him. Around her, he could always lower those high, nearly impenetrable walls he kept up to shield himself from his abusive father.

Right now, though, Mark knew he had no choice but to see her. His wounded arm had to be stabilized. Thank goodness Mattie had taken a training course in administering emergency medical aid just in case one of her students got sick or hurt. Mark hoped they'd taught Mattie how to set a broken arm.

Two days earlier, he'd walked unexpectedly back into her life to warn her that Cardona was going to use the Rocking L road to avoid the US Border Patrol check points and known areas where they looked for drug runners. When Mark had entered her kindergarten class, he'd thought she'd be alone. But Mattie had another woman with her, Tal Culver. Instantly, Mark's radar flashed on because the Culver woman was a helluva lot more than who she seemed to be.

She wore a medical boot on one foot and lower leg, but his operator's senses warned him she was damned dangerous to him. Sensing her, feeling her rock-solid confidence gleaming in her eyes, instantly assessing him like a sniper would, he groaned internally. She looked like she was from the military.

This was Christmastime. Had his best friend Wyatt, who'd been in the Navy SEALs, brought her home with him? Was she also black ops, like Wyatt? Mark would bet money that Tal Culver was all of that—and more. She was potentially dangerous to him and to his undercover work. If she was black ops as he suspected, she could eventually dig into top secret files and be able to reveal what he was really doing—and that just couldn't happen.

This realization stopped him from being more warm and open with Mattie, who had been washing out tempera paint from glass pint jars at the sink when he'd quietly entered the premises. He felt danger around this unknown woman, and was confused about who she was until Mattie introduced her as Wyatt's fiancée. That didn't ease Mark's concern: between her military training and her game face, he felt tense. Plus, he had another set of ears listening to what he wanted to tell Mattie in confidence. He couldn't do it with another set of ears around.

The meeting with Mattie had gone downhill from there. He'd been cold and abrupt, warning her that Cardona was going to drive through the Lockwood ranch property at one corner two nights from now. He'd asked her to warn the Lockwood family. Knowing that Wyatt was home for the holidays from gossip he'd picked up earlier, Mark knew she would get the word to him. Wyatt was an ex-SEAL, and he knew his old friend would decode his words in a heartbeat.

What he didn't want was for Wyatt or anyone else from the Lockwood family to be out in that area when Cardona's men drove his trucks down the road that skirted around the Guadalupe Mountains on their ranch property.

He knew he'd been right when Wyatt had shown up in full battle gear for the fracas. At that point, all Mark was focused on was keeping his friend from being shot by the drug soldiers who would kill Wyatt or anyone else who might interrupt their operation. Mark knew Wyatt wouldn't stand down on this op, that he'd take part in it. Texans didn't take lightly to trespassing on their ranch property and Wyatt was the oldest son in the family. Yeah, he knew Wyatt would show up here to stop Cardona's men. At least, he'd saved his friend's life and Tal would have her fiancé back. Besides, it was Christmastime and only good things should happen now for that family, not bad ones.

Making it to the darkened highway, he began a fast jog toward Van Horn, eight miles away. He could easily make a series of ten-minute miles toward his destination. As a Marine Recon, he was used to carrying a fifty-pound pack on his back while on his missions. All he had to do was get off the highway if he saw headlights coming his way, since Mark did not want to be spotted by any traffic.

Usually at this time of night, there was none. But more US government vehicles could be speeding this way, called in to help with the survivors found in those semi-trucks owned by Cardona.

His heart turned toward Mattie. The least he could do was apologize for his abrupt behavior two days ago. How he ached to see her, to be near her. But to do that could put her and her entire family in danger from Cardona. The drug lord had spies in every Texas town along the border.

Mattie was his touchstone, the one person in his life he could never be without. And yet, he was about to disappear again from her life without an adequate explanation.

How would she react to him banging on her front door in the middle of the night? Would she even let him in? Mark wasn't sure after the debacle at Mattie's kindergarten school with Tal Culver. More than anything, he needed Mattie— more than life. She owned his heart and she didn't even know it.

MATTIE GROANED, HEARING a soft knock at the door of her home. Pushing her red hair away from her face, she sat up in her pink, flannel granny gown. It kept her warm during the winter months and she could turn down the heat in her small, twelve-hundred square foot home to save money. Wiping the sleep from her eyes, she checked the clock. It was 3:15 a.m. Who could be knocking at her front door at this hour?

Something was obviously wrong. She slid her feet into her soft, sheepskin fleece slippers. Trying to wake up—which was never easy without at least two cups of coffee—she hurried through the living room and went to the front door. She looked through the peephole and saw Mark Reuss standing there, his face sweaty and drawn, with that perennial black baseball cap he always wore on his head.

Mark! Mattie quickly turned off the porch light, not wanting anyone to see him standing there. Mattie was often the subject of local gossip. After all, she was twenty-eight years old and no longer married. The townspeople were very family oriented, and often she would be asked if she wanted her own family someday. Of course she did, but with the right man, not the wrong one. Pushing her divorce out of her mind, she quickly opened the door, pushing the screen open.

"Mark?"

"Hey, I'm sorry to wake you at this time of the morning. Can I come in, Mattie? Please?"

"Of course," she murmured, stepping aside. As he passed her, she smelled odd scents reminiscent of gun powder. She had turned on a lamp in the living room, and it gave off just enough light for her to see him clearly. He was wearing a black tactical vest, black pants, and a black shirt. There was dust covering his lower legs. What had he been up to? He was still wearing that beard.

"What happened to you?" she asked, locking the door and turning to face him. She saw him holding his left forearm against his body. His usual, darkly-tanned skin was now pale.

"I was in a rollover accident," he lied. "I

think I've broken my lower arm, Mattie. I know you're an EMT. Can you help me? Then I'll be on my way."

"Your truck rolled over?" she asked, disbelieving.

"Yeah."

She frowned. His story didn't make sense. He was lying to her. Again. She put the lie aside and said, "Let's get you to the bathroom so I can examine your arm." Mattie knew that if his truck had rolled over, a fire truck with an ambulance squad would have been called, and he'd have received help at the scene. Then, they would have brought Mark to their small hospital, if necessary. What had really happened? What was he covering up and not telling her? She remembered his warning from two days ago.

Compressing her lips, she followed him into the bathroom. She'd lived in this house for years. Four months ago, Mark had abruptly walked out of her life. Not that he'd been in it that much since he'd left for the Marine Corps at eighteen and returned home at twenty-eight.

Nine months earlier, he'd finally come home to stay. Then, he'd walked away from her again. He'd taken a job as a wrangler on a nearby ranch and she wondered if he'd been fired from it. Mark hadn't said, but gossip was rife in the town after that. He said El Paso was a place to find a good paying job and he was gone once more.

Mark flipped on the light in the bathroom and moved aside to allow her to pass him. The area was fairly large, with sparkling white tiles on the floor, the room a pale lavender with wispy looking, feminine curtains at the window. Quickly pulling the Velcro open on his tactical vest, he slipped out of it, dropping it to the clean floor. Mattie was gathering several first-aid items out of a nearby cabinet and setting them on the long, white-marble counter where he stood near the water basin.

"Thanks for helping me out," he said gruffly. His black t-shirt was soaked with sweat, clinging to his lean, hard body.

"You need some help getting that long-sleeved shirt off?" she asked, coming over to help him. She could see him trying to favor his left lower arm.

"Yes, thanks," he admitted, allowing her to help ease the shirt off his shoulders. When Mattie came around to his left side, she opened the button on the cuff and gently pulled the fabric off his injured arm. Mark got his first look at the break and heard her swift intake of breath.

"How long ago did this happen?" she asked, leaning over, studying the swollen, bruised area. Her need to touch Mark was still strong, and as she slid her fingers lightly on either side of the break, a frisson of yearning exploded through her.

"About two hours ago," he said.

"I need to examine it more closely, Mark."

He sat down on a nearby stool, placing his arm on the counter to give it some stability. "Go ahead."

"It might be painful," she warned.

"What isn't painful about my life, Mattie?" He lifted his chin, staring into her eyes. "I've had lots of experience in that area."

Her mouth flexed in silent agreement with his statement as she gently palpated the area, feeling him begin to tense. "I know you and Sage had a horrible childhood. As far as I'm concerned, Jeb was a monster."

"He still is," he managed, more pain throbbing up his arm as she slowly began to press the pads of her fingertips along the edge of the swollen tissue.

As careful as she tried to be, Mattie couldn't keep her feelings from spilling over and flooding through her. Just being able to touch Mark made her lower body tremble. She placed her hand on his tense shoulder after the examination. "I think you have a green break, Mark. That means the bone cracked laterally, but didn't actually snap or break the bone in two. I don't feel either of your two, lower-arm bones displaced, either."

"That's good news," he said, slowly opening and closing his hand, feeling more pain from the flexing movement.

She turned. "You need to get it X-rayed to be sure, but you know that."

"Yeah, they taught us EMT-level medicine as Recons," he agreed. "But I'm not ready to do that yet." He stopped, thinking of his next words. "Look, Mattie, I'm here because I trust you. I'll get the X-ray later. I promise."

His gaze followed her as she dug into another drawer, drawing out an air splint. It was a plastic device to stabilize a wound. Mattie would place it around his break as a temporary measure. "This air splint will help you a lot. You also need to take two, eight-hundred milligram tablets of ibuprofen for the swelling, and the pain should begin to recede," she said. Frowning, she added, "But first, I'm going to gently wash your lower arm before I put this on."

"I can do that, Mattie. Just give me a wash rag, put some soap on it, and turn the water on, okay?"

"Sure," she murmured. She'd been eager for another reason to touch him, but Mark was restless and moved around on the stool, always looking warily out the door, waiting . . . watching. For what? For whom?

This had been their problem—Mark never told her anything and she knew he was living in a shadowy world of some kind. She needed to talk to her older brother, Wyatt, about this. He was black ops, too, and might be able to shed some light on why Mark, for the last four months, had disappeared from Van Horn for that truck driver job in El Paso.

Now, Mattie produced a clean washcloth and brought the water to a pleasant temperature, then scrubbed soap into it, and handed it to Mark. He grimaced as he lightly washed the area, including the swollen area around the break.

"Be more gentle with yourself, Mark," she chided, sliding her fingers across his shoulder. Just touching him was a salve to her broken heart.

It wasn't that he'd visited that often while he was still there in town, but he would drop in and see her at the kindergarten at least once a week. How she'd anticipated those few minutes he'd spend with her, even though he treated her as a friend, nothing more.

"Gentle? That's a word of yours I recognize, Mattie." Mark gave her a slight, pained grin as he rinsed his arm beneath the faucet.

Getting a small towel, she said, "Let me do this, okay?" She turned off the faucet, wrapping the towel lightly around his lower arm. "There," she murmured, "now let it dry for a minute and then I'll place the splint around it."

He glanced at the watch on his right wrist. "I need to leave soon, Mattie," he told her firmly, eager to get going.

"You don't have a truck to drive, so where

do you think you're going?" She hated herself when she used logic to let him know that his weak alibi was just that. But didn't she deserve the truth? Anger and frustration flashed in her eyes, and she held his gaze. How she wished she could figure out what he was thinking and feeling!

Mark had been closed up all his life, but Mattie understood why. Jeb, his violent father, had beaten him at least weekly with that belt he wore. She'd seen it happen sometimes, and sobbing, she'd turned and run away, hiding in one of the big barns behind their red-brick ranch house.

"I'll find me a ride," he said, falling silent.

Lifting the towel away, she picked up the splint. "Are you hungry? Thirsty?"

He was so closed up that Mark reminded her of a castle without a draw bridge. If Mattie didn't ask a lot of questions, Mark would say nothing. People just couldn't get close to him. And God knew, she wanted to wrap her arms around him, hold him, and let him know she loved him.

"I am thirsty, yes," he admitted.

"I'll get you some water."

"Thank you, Mattie." He held her worried gaze. "You're a damn good medic. I'll bet your kids can hardly wait to get a scrape so they can have your soothing hands on them."

She closed the Velcro on the splint, smiling a

little. "Half of stopping the hurt is just holding them, kissing their foreheads, and having my arms around them."

"I sure can agree with that form of therapy."

Startled by his statement, she blinked as he stood up. Trying to hide her surprise, she managed, "I have a cotton sling you can wear. That arm needs support. If you let it hang down, all the blood will go into your hand, and your fingers will swell up."

"Right," he murmured. "Got one in one of those drawers?" He gestured toward them.

"I do. Two of everything." She bent down to retrieve a package.

"You're like the SEALs," he said. "They want two of everything. 'One is none, two is one,' is their motto, and in their world, they're right."

She opened the packet, pulling the soft, triangular piece of cotton cloth out of it. "Wyatt taught me that right after he graduated out of BUDs. The SEALs had it correct. You were black ops, too. You probably had two of everything, I'll bet." She moved in front of him, pulling the sling into position.

"No, I traveled light, Mattie. Maybe a thirty to fifty-pound pack on my back. I'd be out for weeks, scrounging off the land doing my job."

You still are, she thought, but resisted saying it. "There," she murmured, lifting her arms away, so close to his body she could feel the heat rolling off of him. Mark lifted his arm and slid it carefully into the sling.

She stepped away. "How does it feel now?" she asked.

"Much better." He gave her a tender look. "You're a healer, Mattie. You always will be. I really appreciate you. Thanks for this."

"Come on," she urged, moving past him, "let's head for the kitchen and I'll get you that water." If she didn't move, she'd try to get him to stay so she could find out what was going on in his life. Even Sage didn't know what he was up to, and that worried Mattie even more.

Aware of her shapeless granny gown, she tried to put thoughts of vanity aside and moved toward the kitchen. Nervously, she pushed her fingers through her long, shoulder length hair, feeling like a drudge.

Normally, she wore light makeup and kept her hair as orderly as she could, given its natural curl. How she wished she had on a nicer nightie right now instead of this frumpy granny gown!

Glancing out the window, she saw snow-flakes tapping against it. Retrieving a glass from the cupboard, she filled it with water, and when she turned, Mark was standing a few feet away, an unfamiliar look on his face. There was no mistaking it, and she almost let the glass slip through her fingers as she registered pure, naked desire in his eyes.

"Here . . ." she managed, her fingers connecting with his as she passed the glass to him.

"Thanks," he said roughly.

Mattie watched him drink thirstily, eagerly, until the water was gone.

"More?"

"Yes, please." He handed it back to her.

"You're going to miss that left arm of yours," she said wryly, turning and filling the glass once more. "A green break takes four to six weeks to heal. You can't use it, Mark, and if you try, you could snap the bone in two."

"Okay, Doc," he intoned, a brief smile on his face. Then it was gone.

Mattie could see the outline of his hard, male body beneath the damp t-shirt he wore. His chest was wide, his belly hard and flat, his hips narrow. He was a very sensual guy, Mattie observed. She wondered if he was aware of his charisma and how it affected women. Probably not.

He'd been a joy to watch as a cornerback during Saturday night football games back in high school, and he'd become one of the school's heroes because he'd helped his team get a state championship during his junior year. Girls HAD drooled all over him after that. But despite their interest, he always chose Mattie to hang out with.

"That tasted good, Mattie," he said, handing the glass to her. He glanced up, looking at the clock above them. "Well, I'd better get going."

"Can't I drive you somewhere, Mark?" Instantly, the look in his eyes flattened and became indecipherable.

"No. It's four a.m., Mattie. I know you have school tomorrow at seven." He reached out, surprising her by touching a curled strand near her cheek. "Go back to bed and don't worry about me. I'm just a bad penny in your life. You never know when I'll turn up. Hey, get some sleep, okay?"

The moment his finger grazed her cheek, easing the strand away from near her eye, she fought back a desperate hunger for more. He knew from their high school days together how she felt about him, but since returning home, Mattie assumed she was still just a good friend, even though she wanted so much more. But he wouldn't let her inside those walls he'd built. She wasn't sure he even saw her as anything more than friend. Rallying, she gave him a tender look.

"Okay, I will. Do you need anything else? I have some protein bars in the drawer over there."

"Nah, I'm fine." He took a few steps away from her, then turned and said, "I'm sorry, Mattie. I just seem to come to you when I'm hurt so you can patch me up and send me off again. You deserve so much more than that. Take care of yourself, okay?"

# CHAPTER 2

*December 24*

"WHAT DO YOU think, Wyatt?" Mattie asked her brother the next evening. Tal, his fiancée, had come with him. Mattie had made them supper and told them about Mark's unexpected appearance. Tal listened closely, saying little, but Mattie could see there was a lot going on in her head by the look in her eyes and the set of her mouth.

Wyatt cut the apple pie Mattie had made for them at the kitchen counter. "My guess is that he's in some kind of black-ops activity, Mattie."

"But on which side?" she asked, holding up a china plate with pink cactus flowers painted around its edges.

"Good question," Tal said, standing up from the table. "I'll get us coffee and we can go to the living room, all right, Mattie?"

"Yes, that would be great, Tal. Thanks." She turned and looked at her brother. Wyatt had confided to her that Mark had saved his life last night even though he'd broken his arm. She remembered Mark had given her a warning two days earlier and said, "Wyatt, Mark warned us not to go to that corner of our ranch. So who is he working for?"

Wyatt's mouth pursed and he put two more pieces of pie on two more plates. "That's what I can't figure out right now, Mattie. Mark warned you to stay away from that area, so for me, given the way he was dressed last night, he could be working for that drug lord, Cardona. His base of operation is in Ciudad Juarez, Mexico. Mark wasn't with the government forces that I was with last night. He was working on the other side. I don't like saying this because I don't want to believe Mark would do that kind of illegal activity."

Gasping a little, Mattie stared up at her brother. He didn't look happy about it, either.

"Come on," Wyatt urged her gently, picking up two of the plates. "Let's go have our dessert in the living room and we can discuss it further in there."

Mattie numbly nodded and picked up the last piece of pie. Following him, she saw that Tal, even wearing that medical boot on her injured foot, had managed to get three filled mugs of coffee on the coffee table in front of the couch.

Tal sat down with Wyatt on the gold velour couch and Mattie took the overstuffed chair opposite them. They looked worried.

"You're both black ops. Tal, I know you were a Marine Corps sniper and a captain, and Wyatt was a SEAL and a sniper. What are you two putting together about Mark's disappearance and his visit last night with a broken arm?"

Wyatt cut into his pie with a fork and glanced to his right, meeting Tal's shadowed gaze. "Well," he drawled, "my guess is that he's either gone over to the dark side or he's working undercover for our government and can't tell anyone that's what he's doing. He's sworn to secrecy."

"The dark side?" Tal asked, her thin black brows knitting as she studied Wyatt. "Why use that term? It's not the military."

"It's a long story, Tal," Mattie said. I'll give you the shorter version. "'Dark side' was a code word among the Lockwood and Reuss kids as we grew up together. Mark got the hell beaten out of him for nearly fifteen years by his old man, Jeb Reuss. His father kept telling him that he was from the dark side, someone who would stain the life of everyone he met. He convinced the kid that only bad things would happen to people when he showed up."

Tal grimaced. "What a bastard, doing that number on his own child!"

Wyatt sat back, enjoying his pie. "There's a lot of stuff you don't know, darlin,' about this area. Otherwise it wouldn't surprise you that Jeb Reuss is actually the black cloud in everyone's life, not just Mark's. My father went to court with three different lawsuits against the guy while I was growing up. Jeb is a bully and he takes what he wants. He doesn't ask and doesn't care if it's someone else's property. He's been in and out of jail practically every year. And on top of that, he's an alcoholic."

"Yes, and a mean, abusive one," Mattie added bitterly. "Mark bears scars on his back and hips from when his dad hit him with that thick leather belt he always wore."

"Good God," Tal muttered, disbelief in her voice. "Where was his mother?"

"Dead," Wyatt said flatly. "She died when Sage, the second child, was born. Jeb blamed his daughter for his wife's death, of course. He was always good at assigning blame to everyone else but himself."

"Yes," Mattie breathed quietly, "Jeb was verbally, emotionally, and physically abusive toward Mark and Sage."

"Mark did everything he could to protect Sage from that sick bastard," Wyatt growled. "He took the beatings meant for her and he'd always challenge Jeb, making himself the target so Sage could escape."

Tal blinked. "This sounds horrible, Wyatt. Where was law enforcement? Why wasn't Jeb thrown into prison for what he did to his children?"

"Because Jeb was smart enough to put bruises on Mark where they wouldn't be seen by his teachers," Mattie said. "And both sets of grandparents were not here to help or protect those two children."

"Mark's grandparents on his father's side, were dead. Their mother's family was back in Maine. They hated Jeb and never came out for a visit, so Sage and Mark grew up without ever meeting them. It's heartbreaking."

"Is Jeb still alive?" Tal wondered.

"Oh, yeah," Wyatt muttered. "He's too mean a snake to die young."

"Well, who's running the Reuss ranch, then?"

"Sage is," Mattie said. "Jeb suffered a debilitating stroke five years ago. Mark was in the Marine Corps, deployed to Afghanistan when it happened. He never took medical leave to come home and see his father, but you can't blame him for that. Jeb still lives on the ranch, but Sage brought it back from the edge of bankruptcy and made it successful. Now, she raises Brangus cattle."

"And he still lives on the ranch with her?" Tal demanded.

"Yes," Wyatt said between bites. "There's a

small house about half a mile away from the main ranch house. It's a single-story, red-brick home. Jeb lives there with a male caregiver Sage pays to assist him. She won't have anything to do with her father."

Mattie sought to reassure Tal. "Sage and I have always been the best of friends, and she refuses to do anything for her father except pay his medical bills and see that he's comfortable. She won't visit him or talk to him. Instead, all communications go through Frank, the helper who takes care of Jeb."

Tal pushed a bit of pie around on her plate with her fork, frowning down at it. "Sounds like a pretty dysfunctional family, if you ask me."

"It is," Wyatt agreed. "All four of us kids were friends with Mark and Sage while we were growing up. They spent most of their time here at our ranch whenever they could. They wanted to get as far away from Jeb and his violent anger as possible. Often, my mother would invite them to stay for dinner, especially in the summertime. Because everyone knew Jeb's drinking schedule, we'd drive them back to their ranch after dark, when Jeb had passed out on the sofa. Mark and Sage could then experience a quiet, uneventful night."

Tal sighed and picked at her pie, upset by what she was hearing. "And yet, Mark saved your life last night, Wyatt. He's not all bad as everyone seems to make him out to be."

Nodding, Wyatt finished off his pie, setting the plate on the coffee table. "Mark was a Recon Marine, Tal, black ops. He was in Afghanistan for five deployments, just like us. The Marine Corps does a serious background check on anyone applying for the Recons, as you know, and Mark passed in flying colors. He was never the dark presence his old man made him out to be to the people of Van Horn. Sometimes, I'd see Mark at Bagram and we'd sit, chow down, and have a beer together."

"Does Mark believe he's a bad person?" Tal wondered.

Mattie moved her hands nervously in her lap. "Yes, he believes it, Tal, and it just kills me. He's the kindest, most gentle man I know."

"He didn't look that way when I saw him at your kindergarten class," she said. "He was on guard and looked pretty uptight. I could tell he didn't trust me at all."

"He was jumpy," Mattie agreed. "I could tell he wished you weren't there because he wanted to tell me something, but I don't know what it was."

"You mean more than what he actually did tell you?" Wyatt asked.

"Yes." She shrugged and gave them a helpless look. "It was just a gut feeling, Wyatt, that's all. It was nothing he said."

"He's seems to be a man of few words," Tal said. "He was wary of me. I sensed he knew I was black ops, too, because you tend to recognize your own kind by just being in the same general vicinity with them."

Wyatt slid her a warm glance. "I sure did with you."

Tal snorted. "It wasn't exactly love at first sight with you, Lockwood."

Giving her a cocky grin, he preened. "No, that's true, but I wore you down with my good ole Texas boy ways."

Mattie smiled. "You two are good for each other."

Tal raised an eyebrow. "We didn't realize it at first, believe me."

"Oh," Wyatt gloated, "I knew from the gitgo, darlin'. I just had to be patient until you figured it all out in your beautiful mind. After all, you were pretty busy being the assistant CO of a sniper group at Bagram."

"You were certainly a serious distraction for me, Lockwood."

Chuckling, he said, "Yes, the best kind. Don't you agree?"

Mattie loved their back-and-forth, and felt all her tension melt away listening to their playful banter. She could tell her brother deeply loved Tal and vice versa. Inwardly, she wished with all her heart and soul that she and Mark could have a similar relationship.

But that wasn't going to happen.

"Mattie?" Wyatt said, interrupting her thoughts. "When we get back to Artemis in Alexandria in early January, I'm going to do some snooping around about Mark. If he's undercover, it's certainly deep, which means I have to find the right guy who'll give me more than a stonewall answer."

"Remember, Wyatt, as a SEAL, you taught the whole Lockwood clan about what 'top secret' means," Mattie said drily. "I know I'm a civilian, and I know there's a lot I don't know about the military, brother. But if you could find out what Mark's doing, I'd sleep a lot better at night."

MARK DIDN'T THINK the garbage he'd sunk into could get any deeper, but it was going that direction. He'd holed up in an abandoned warehouse on the other side of Van Horn. Needing sleep before he figured out what to do next, he'd awakened near noon, feeling cold, curled up in a small room to protect himself from the drafts of the aluminum building that had seen better days.

Suddenly, his cell phone rang. Pulling it out of his back jean's pocket, Mark saw the number flash on his cell and knew it was his DEA handler, Gordon Hilber. Cursing softly, he answered it.

"Where the hell are you, Reuss?"

"I'm in a warehouse at the western end of Van Horn, laying low," he snarled back. Hilber was one of those control freaks who had never done undercover work but liked to make others miserable by acting superior.

"I've been calling for hours. The multi-agency assault on Cardona's trucks was a complete success. Where the hell did you go? What are you doing in Van Horn? You know you shouldn't be there."

Sitting up, he rested his broken arm against his belly. Mark had taken off the sling earlier so he could try to sleep. He'd managed to catch some shuteye, but it had been light, restless sleep. Now, he was irritable but he told Hilber what had happened, leaving Mattie out of the equation. He would protect her at all costs.

"Your Jeep overturned?"

"Yeah, so I don't have wheels." He gave Hilber the address of the warehouse where he could be picked up.

"Has Cardona tried contacting you?"

"Not yet. Things are probably in disarray. He's going to be pissed off about those three trucks taken by those agencies. He was expecting this run to be smooth and uneventful trip across the border."

"I'm worried that Cardona will kill you if you show up."

"Why?"

"Because all his men have either been killed, wounded, or put into custody at the assault site last night."

"Hell, he won't know where I am. He has no idea exactly what happened last night. Did any of his soldiers get away?"

"None of them," Hilber said, sounding satisfied. Then, his tone changed to one of concern. "What about you? Have you gone to a hospital to get your arm checked out?"

"No. There's no way I'm exposing myself here in Van Horn. I don't want Cardona finding out I was here, and then sending a truck full of drug soldiers to shoot up the town or the hospital because it's where I used to live."

"But Cardona doesn't know you're from Van Horn. Your identification and name are fake."

"Even so, I didn't want to risk it," he said, suddenly weary. He hadn't eaten since yesterday before the attack and needed some water, but there wasn't any in the warehouse.

"I've decided to pull you from this operation, Reuss. You're done. We'll find something else for you."

Anger surged through Mark, his fingers tightening around the cell phone. "The only reason I got in bed with you bastards was to save my friend's family and their lives."

"Yes, and you did that. They're in the Witness Protection Program, long gone, their names changed. Cardona will never find them, so you did good on that one, Reuss. But I'm afraid Cardona will suspect you if you show up without any of his other soldiers."

"I thought the same thing, which is why I holed up here."

"Look, I want you to get to a hospital."

"I'm fine. I've had worse injuries before, Hilber."

"Then I'm sending a car from El Paso to pick you up."

"When you do," Mark growled, "I'm quitting the DEA. I'm finished." There was dead silence over the phone line.

"I want my fucking life back. Going undercover guarantees I'll never have one. I did this to get my Marine friend out of Cardona's network, and that's been accomplished."

"So what will you do?" Hilber demanded, his voice shaking with fury.

"Go home and start my life all over," Mark said. "Cardona doesn't know my real name or where I live."

"That's true, but we need you, Mark."

He heard the wheedling in Hilber's voice and he snarled, "I need a life, dammit. I spent ten years in the Marine Corps. My time with the

DEA is enough. I'm not interested in what you want to offer me. Get my papers in order by the time I reach El Paso. I'm quitting. Send a car to pick me up and make it fast. I'm tired, cold, and hungry. I'll send you the GPS."

Clicking off the cell after sending his location, Mark sat with his back against a wall. The place was musty, with cobwebs and dust everywhere. His stomach growled. It would be so easy to walk to that café, José's Diner, and grab a hot breakfast. His mind whirled with options. It would take a few hours for a DEA car to come to Van Horn and pick him up here at this warehouse. He could walk the quarter mile and get a hot breakfast. But he knew José, and he knew he'd be recognized. What lies would he tell the owner? And what if Mattie showed up for breakfast?

Rubbing his gritty face, he closed his eyes, trying to think. The pain in his arm was lessening and he was grateful. Damn it, his poor excuse for a father had been right about him. All he brought others was misery and suffering. He'd seen how Mattie felt about him earlier this morning. She never could hide her deep affection for him.

Suddenly, he was overcome with sadness. He felt alone, with nothing to anchor him. Thanks to the Marine Corps, he'd had stability and purpose, and he'd begun to feel that he was valuable to others, not a curse or underfoot any longer.

Slowly, he was dislodging the poison his father had planted within him. But it was an uphill battle, and now, he was reminded that he couldn't escape his past.

But then, there was Mattie. His heart opened as he visualized her sweet face, her freckles, her red hair that was just as wild and free as she was. Just seeing her filled him with peace—it always had. He wished he could tell her how much she meant to him. Could he ever? In Van Horn, he'd been a troublemaker throughout school, and his reputation had followed him into adulthood.

Only Mattie had vehemently, passionately spoken up in his defense. She was a fighter, loyal as they came, and she didn't care whom she confronted when it came to him and his stained reputation.

How he loved her.

Rubbing his chest, he felt a pain of loss that was so deep, he couldn't even begin to give it words. His innocence had been lost after his years growing up with Mattie. She'd nourished his soul with her smile, her laughter, the mischievous glint in her eyes, and her devotion. The two innocents had dreamed together when in high school about their futures. Mark was unsure of his, but Mattie wasn't. She had a very active imagination, sharing with him what she wanted out of life: a home, a husband, and lots of children.

But none of those felt possible to Mark. After living with Jeb, such dreams felt unreal, impossible even to imagine. Mark couldn't dream the same dreams that Mattie had. After all, she had parents who loved her and the rest of her siblings. That was why he and Sage had been pulled, like magnets, to the Lockwood ranch next door and had spent so much time with the four of them, loving every minute.

Mark hated going home at night to his drunken father passed out on the couch. His whole world revolved around protecting Sage. She was so beautiful and innocent. Mark remembered that, even at age ten, he'd thought Sage was perfect.

When his father began looking at her intently, and not at all like a father should, Sage had felt it, and so had he. His life during those first eighteen years had been a hot mess.

Now, gazing at his surroundings in the quiet warehouse, hearing the wind lift some of the aluminum siding around it, the creaks, the metal sounds, he felt as if he had been totally catapulted to another planet. The only thing that made sense in his crazy life was Mattie Lockwood. He'd kissed her when they were juniors in high school. He wanted to protect her, and himself, even though he felt unworthy of someone like her. How could he dream of having her when he was such a messed-up loser?

Tipping his head back against the wall, Mark let himself return to his happy times with Mattie. This was a special moment, since he rarely had time to do so while undercover. He had to be vigilant to prevent the Cardona gang from finding out he was an enemy in their midst. Now, he had the gift of time.

Mattie was less than a mile away from where he'd taken refuge. What would she think if he walked back into her life at some point after he came back to Van Horn after leaving the DEA? She'd always welcomed him, always treated him like a good friend, whether he felt he deserved it or not.

His mind spun with options, choices, and confusion over what to do next. He knew that first, he had to get to the DEA headquarters in El Paso. It was there he'd adopted his fake name, a beard, and gone underground. Now, for some reason, he felt freer than he had in a long time because he'd told Hilbert he was quitting.

Where should he go? Mark knew one thing for sure—he wasn't going back to his family ranch. There were several other ranches in the area, and maybe he could apply for a job as a wrangler with one of them.

Sure, fat chance! Everyone knew he was a troublemaker. Wearily rubbing his face, he knew he was at a crossroads in his life. But which way should he go? What to do? If Mattie were here, he could talk to her about it. She always had sensible ideas and a practical approach to life. God, he wished he could see her right now!

# CHAPTER 3

*January 24*

MATTIE REGRETTED THAT she'd rejected her family's invitation to join them for dinner, but she knew she would have been poor company. When she had black moments like these, they would drown her in a sea of sadness she couldn't rise above. Usually, she'd have an episode after Mark had unexpectedly appeared—not that she blamed him for her depressions.

Mark had always brought out her deepest emotions. During their most recent encounter a month ago, she had dressed his broken arm and then, right on script, she'd watched him disappear again. After that, there had been no contact. And once again, his secrecy was getting her down.

Five months earlier, he'd suddenly quit his wrangling job at the Cavanaugh Ranch just outside Van Horn, and told everyone he was leaving for El Paso. Apparently, he had found a new job as a truck driver, and he'd warned everyone not to expect to hear from him. He'd been as good as his word, which Mattie hadn't liked one bit!

Outside it was cold, a mixture of rain and ice pellets hitting her windows. Kindergarten would probably be cancelled tomorrow due to the icy, dangerous weather sweeping across western Texas. She sat down in her home office to create next week's lesson plans and fun projects for her classes.

Mattie tried not to think about what Wyatt had told her last week when she'd called him at his office, pleading with him to tell her if Mark was all right.

His theory that Mark might be involved in the drug trade had alarmed her, but Wyatt had pointed out this was pure conjecture. He didn't know anything for sure—just that Mark Reuss had been off the grid since he'd gone off to El Paso.

Mattie shivered as she heard the wind buffeting her house, reminding her that a cold front was coming through tonight and tomorrow morning. The desert landscape here in Texas badly needed rain. She sighed and pulled out her lesson plans from the spreadsheet on her Mac desktop computer.

At least preparing for her classes was doing

something positive, and she knew her kids would love all the hands-on activities she had gleefully planned for them. That was an upper and lifted her spirits a bit.

The sound of the doorbell shook her out of her reverie. Frowning, she looked up toward the hall. Who could that be? She knew her family was going to begin their dinner over at the Rocking L Ranch about now. Looking at her watch, she saw that it was eight p.m.

Pushing her office chair back, she smoothed down her jeans and quickly walked out into the hall.

Curious, she looked through the peephole. It was Mark! He was standing on her steps, uneasily shifting back and forth and getting rained on. His black Stetson and a heavy sheepskin coat were soaked, his face wet from having been pelted with rain.

Instantly, her heart began to pound. Gripping the knob, she opened the door.

"Mark!" she exclaimed. "What are you doing here?" She was shocked to see that he was now clean-shaven.

"I know it's late, Mattie, but I need to see you." His voice was low and gruff.

"Of course, come in," she said, stepping aside. Her gaze went from his glistening face to the dark splotches along the shoulders of his sheepskin coat. Then, looking beyond him, she saw he had a silver Ford pickup parked outside her white picket fence. At least this time he had wheels.

"Thanks," he said, stepping on her large, bristly floor mat just inside the house. He carefully wiped his boots off.

Mattie locked the door and slowly turned toward Mark. The exhaustion she saw on his face, however, was both a bad sign and a good one. She hated that he was pushing himself too hard, which made her worry. But she was grateful that he was willing to share his true state of mind, which he normally hid from her and everyone else. She knew he trusted her, and that he'd turn up when he needed her to bail him out for some reason or another, like tending to his wounded arm. And she was always willing to be there for him. It was the hasty departures afterward that made her sad, and the game face he'd put on that created a barrier between them.

"How's your arm doing?" she asked, gesturing toward it. She saw him pull his hands out of his pockets.

"It's pretty good. You were right, Mattie. It was a green break closed fracture." Looking around, he asked, "Am I coming at a bad time?"

"No, I'm here alone. The weather is so awful, everyone's staying in. I'm sure they'll cancel school tomorrow morning."

He nodded, his eyes showing concern.

"Yeah, this weather is a bitch. No one in their right mind should be out in this stuff tonight."

Mattie hated that he never called ahead, always assuming she'd be around for him. Would he once again come and go in a few minutes like his usual routine? "What brings you here, Mark? I never see you unless you want something from me. You dropped out of sight after your broken arm, and no one's heard from you since."

He winced at her sharp tone and avoided her eyes for a moment, his jaw working. "I guess I had that coming. I'm here because I quit the trucking job I had in El Paso and I'm coming home to Van Horn." His voice grew thick with emotion. "And first, I wanted to see you, Mattie. To come by and thank you for all you did for me the last time we saw each other." He took off his Stetson, running his long, calloused fingers through his short, black hair.

Surprised, Mattie said, "Oh. I-I didn't know you'd quit that job . . . whatever it was . . ."

The corners of his mouth stretched a little as he held her gaze. "You're the first person to know I'm back here for good. And I'm not here because I need something from you this time, Mattie. You've always been a loyal friend, despite me being who I am. I just wanted to drop by and say 'thanks'."

"You're home? For good?"

"Yeah, pretty much."

Swallowing hard, Mattie could barely resist throwing her arms around Mark. He'd been a shadow in her life since he'd left the military nearly a year ago. Wanting to believe his words, she asked, "What does 'pretty much' mean, Mark?"

"Well, first I need to find a job. I also need to find a place to live and all that."

"You could go home to your ranch and live with Sage," she suggested. Oops! That was a mistake!. She saw his mouth harden and knew he was processing unhappy memories. How she wished she could take back her words!

"You know I can't do that, Mattie. When I left for the Corps at eighteen, I promised myself I'd never step foot back on that ranch until Jeb had died. And the bastard is still alive."

"Yes, it's true," Mattie agreed. "He is alive, and he's still making everyone miserable on the ranch. But through it all, Sage has brought the place back to life. It's financially solvent now."

He settled the hat back on his head, stuffing his hands back into the coat once more.

Changing the subject, he ventured, "I was wondering if you've heard of any ranches around Van Horn that might be looking to hire another wrangler?"

Mattie suddenly brightened. "Well, as a matter of fact, my dad told me the other day that he needed one."

Mark's eyes lit up. "Really?"

"Yes. Hank lost one of his best and oldest vaqueros, Pepe, who had to move back to Mexico because his parents weren't well."

"Hey, I remember Pepe growing up. He's a good man and a helluva wrangler."

Mattie drew in a breath, let it out, and said, "Let's talk it over at dinner. Have you eaten, Mark?"

"No, not since this morning. I've been traveling all day through this damned cold front." He frowned, gesturing toward the door. "Black ice is everywhere on the roads between El Paso and here. It was really slow going and I saw a lot of accidents along the route."

"That's why I'm not leaving the house to do anything until the storm passes tomorrow around noon," agreed Mattie. "But we can still have a good dinner. I have some leftover pot roast, potatoes, carrots, celery, and a good gravy. Interested?"

He hesitated, looking deep into her eyes. "Do you really want me here, Mattie?"

Mattie shot him a disbelieving look. How could he ask that of her? He immediately felt like a jerk and looked away, riding his own downward trajectory. He knew that Mattie cared for him as a friend, but she looked downright insulted. Heck, he'd feel that way too if she had said that to him!

"Of course I do," she sputtered, indignant

that he'd even suggested such a thing. "We've been friends forever, Mark Reuss! You know that!" She saw relief come to his eyes and he grimaced, giving her an apologetic look.

"I feel like I've always been a bad penny, showing up at odd times in your life, Mattie. I've caused you nothing but frustration whenever I'm around you. I never want to do that to you. You deserve a lot better than me walking in and out of your life again."

"How about if you let me decide that?" she shot back. "Quit making assumptions and let me put some meat on your bones. Follow me."

MARK WAS SO relieved he couldn't speak as he silently followed her into the kitchen. He'd hung up his coat and hat on a wooden peg near the front door. The family area was open concept, well-lit, and very homey. Mark felt that it reflected Mattie's warm, bustling energy, and he loved being here.

Mattie was the most appealing woman he'd ever met. She was just perfect as far as he was concerned, all five feet, seven inches tall, and curvy in all the right places. Tonight she wore a pair of jeans, a purple, long-sleeved sweater, and sneakers. The sway of her hips tempted his body to come back to life, and he tried to keep his physical response under control.

Mattie was a rancher's daughter, an outdoors woman and very capable in every way. He loved her—and always had. That had been the one constant in his life, the only good one. She represented hope to Mark, something he had rarely experienced in his life. Mattie inspired him, but he was afraid to grasp it after having had "you're a curse to everyone who knows you" drilled into him by his father. That, among other reasons, was why he'd chosen black ops as a profession—to fade away into the background, to live in the shadows, to hide his shameful past.

One of his most precious memories was the day he'd met Mattie in the first grade. Mattie had bounced into Miss Harper's first-grade class at the Van Horn Elementary School. She wore a pair of denim overalls, and a bright-pink tee that complemented her coverlet of freckles.

Her red hair, even then, had a mind of its own. The strands were trapped in a set of girlish pigtails and the ends were tied with pink, satin ribbons. Later, he would see her unhappily try to tame that wild hair of hers, but it was curly hair, so it did what it wanted.

Mark had sat in the back of the room, choosing a desk hidden in a shadow, trying to ignore the throbbing pain along his rear where his father had struck him with a belt earlier that morning.

Magically, just seeing Mattie skip into the

small classroom, he forgot his misery and pain. She was like a blinding, beautiful beam of sunlight, transporting him to a different reality. Her smile, so friendly and genuine, made him feel good inside. His attention was always on her throughout their first-grade year, but Mark was too shy to say 'hello' or introduce himself. After all, he was only a shadow, not a whole person.

At quiet moments, which weren't often, he would resurrect his tender image of Mattie as a child. Then, he would visualize her today and his heart would stir, wanting her, wanting to be close to her, wanting so many things that had never been initiated. But he told himself that they were just dreams—broken dreams turned to dust.

The memories poured through Mark now as he sat down at Mattie's rectangular maple table. It had been in her family since the 1850s, when they first came West and began homesteading this area. Everything in her home was from the past, and that alone made him feel good.

"Can I help you at all?" he offered.

"Just sit there and relax," she suggested, opening up the fridge. She turned around to meet his eyes. "How hungry are you?"

He almost said, I'm starving for you, Mattie. I'd love to put my arms around you and haul you into my bed and never let you go. But he didn't. Clearing his throat, he said, "Pretty darn hungry, actually."

Her lips lifted a little. "Like a wrangler hungry after busting his hump for eight hours riding and repairing fence line?"

His mouth curved. "Yeah, that kind of hungry."

Nodding, she got busy pulling out different plastic containers and placing them on the granite counter nearby. "Looks like you've dropped a few pounds, Mark. Let's start with dinner to put some back on, okay?"

Mark nodded, folding his hands on the table, pleased that Mattie cared about his well-being. "That job was pretty stressful, and kept me on the move all the time."

Of course he couldn't tell Mattie that he'd been an undercover drug agent for the DEA. But he didn't want to lie to her, either. He hated doing that because most of his adult life, he'd been living in secrecy. First, he'd done top-secret work in the Marine Corps, and then, in the last five months, with the DEA.

As she pulled down her favorite floral dinner plates, she surprised him by saying "You know, I still remember back in school the time Jeb had beaten you with his belt just before you got on the bus." Cutting some thick slices of beef and transferring it to the plate, she went on, "I couldn't figure out why you couldn't eat your lunch on days like that. Then, when you told me, I understood. You were too upset emotionally to feel hungry." She frowned, hands hovering over the roast beef. "Were you in some kind of trouble over the last five months, Mark? Is that why you stopped eating again and lost so much weight?"

Uneasy, he lowered his lashes and looked down at his tightly clasped hands for a moment. "You been talking to Wyatt?"

She laughed lightly and moved to the container with the veggies in it. "Yes. Does it show?"

"Sort of," he muttered, scowling.

"I told Wyatt that you came here with a broken arm the night afterward. He and Tal had come over for dinner and I told them what happened." She twisted her head around, meeting his narrowed gaze. "I had to ask him what the heck was going on with you."

"And Wyatt's in the black-ops business with Artemis Security," Mark finished.

She poured the gravy over the beef and potatoes, then popped the plate into the microwave. "I had to ask someone, Mark, since you never tell me anything."

His conscience twinging, he nodded, debating what he'd tell her. Mattie was the kind of woman he could confide in, and God knew, he wanted to do exactly that. But he feared that someday it might make her a target, and he wasn't about to ever do that.

She noted his hesitation and said, "Want some butterscotch cream pie later? Got pecans as a topping over it. It's freshly made. I've got whipped cream, too."

His mouth watered. He was starved for good ole Texas home cooking. The last five months had been hell on Earth for him. "Sure, if it's not too much trouble, Mattie." He saw her roll her eyes, that little girl grin creeping across her lips.

"Oh, you are such a shadow in my life, Mark Reuss!"

He could hear the lilt of happiness in her tone as she went back to the fridge and pulled out the pie. Mattie was actually happy he was here! That shocked him because his last meeting with her, when Tal Culver was present just before Christmas, hadn't gone well at all. That was another thing he loved about Mattie—her ability to forgive and move on. She never held a vengeful thought or wanted to get even with someone who had hurt her, either—not like him.

"Are you getting ready to go back to kindergarten after this ice front passes?" he asked. He knew Mattie's schedule well because he'd kept up with her life while he was away in the Corps. Sage had always filled him in when they had their Skype talks and exchanged emails. He knew that Sage had somehow sensed he loved her. Mark didn't know how, but Sage was amazingly psychic.

He raptly watched Mattie cut the pie for him. He was a sucker for a woman who could cook, and warm, lovable Mattie hit all the marks. His mother, Migisi, had been a full-blooded Chippewa Indian and had died birthing Sage when he was only two years old.

Mark had no memories of her, only a few photos that he treasured. Neither he nor Sage had known a woman's nurturing, maternal care, or her love, as a consequence. Instead, Jeb's out-of-control anger, his alcoholism, and his abuse had darkened their lives.

Watching Mattie move efficiently back and forth in the kitchen, he ached for her. She was his dream woman, the only female he'd dared to dream about. She had stolen his heart since the first grade, and still held it—unknowingly—in her hands.

And now, Mark thought, I'm home again, like the proverbial bad penny showing up in her life once more. He wanted to stay in Van Horn and make a life for himself, but could he? He had thought he could after leaving the military, but five months ago the DEA had contacted him asking for his help on a special undercover mission.

Prior to that, he had been working at the Cavenaugh Ranch as a wrangler, making ends meet. He had lived in a bunkhouse with five other men, but found himself having a tough time making the transition from military to civilian life again. It was tougher than he'd expected because of his frequent PTSD symptoms.

He was now twenty-nine and lonely as hell. Wolfishly, he watched Mattie with a hungry gaze, remembering how upset she'd been when they were eighteen and he'd boarded the bus in Van Horn for El Paso. She'd looked as if he'd gutted her. And he had, emotionally, but he'd been just as devastated as he watched her from the back window while the bus pulled away.

And now he was back. Again. What he wanted and what life gave him were probably aimed in two different directions. He wanted Mattie for life, but he knew he was a poor bet. Mattie deserved someone other than the dark bastard who would appear in her life, only to disappear again.

# CHAPTER 4

MATTIE PUT A plate of steaming food before Mark and watched as he ate like a starving animal. Her heart swelled with happiness as she watched him relax, his shoulders easing, his strained expression slowly being replaced by one of deep pleasure as he appreciatively gulped down her food.

As he finished, Mattie left her cup of coffee on the table and went to the refrigerator to retrieve dessert. No longer depressed, she felt a thrumming joy so deep and pure, she allowed herself to flow along with the sense of joy enveloping her.

She knew it was all about Mark being here at long last. They had been inseparable as childhood buddies, and had done everything together. Their joy at being together would only be marred by her discovery of a new bruise on his body when his father would beat him, bringing her to tears. In fact, Mattie lost track of how many times she discovered a bruise or a place where his skin had been torn open. His wounds were always hidden by his jeans or the long-sleeved shirts he wore— Jeb made sure of that.

As she turned to bring Mark his pie, she froze for a moment. He was sitting in the chair, staring hard at her, a hungry look in his eyes. At her age, she knew that look. Swallowing hard, she brought over two pieces of pie, setting one plate in front of him and one on her side of the table.

"Thanks," he mumbled, his expression changing to one of gratitude. "Dinner was great, Mattie. You're such a fine cook," he told her between huge bites of the sweet concoction.

Again, he ate as if he'd been deprived of decent food for months. Mattie wanted to ask him what kind of job he'd had that had turned him into a gaunt version of the man she'd known for years. Even his cheeks had hollowed out, indicating his severe weight loss. She didn't feel like eating, her feelings tamping down her hunger, but forced herself to do so anyway.

"That was damned good pie, Mattie. Thank you."

She warmed beneath his compliment as he stood and picked up all the empty dishes. "You're welcome. Hey, you don't have to do that, Mark. I can clear the table in a minute. Come sit and talk to me?"

"A long time ago, while eating at a certain ten-year-old girl's ranch house, I was told that the cleaning crew consisted of those who hadn't done the cooking."

She chuckled. "Guilty as charged. I guess I figured your mom had taught you that rule." She saw his eyes grow sad for a moment. "I know you still miss her," she said softly. "Growing up without a mother is something I just can't begin to imagine and how it impacted you and Sage."

In response, Mark walked over to the coffee dispenser and picked up the pot, bringing it to the table. "Want a warm-up?" he asked, holding it near her empty cup.

"Yes, thanks," Mattie whispered, caught off guard by his thoughtfulness. Automatically, she inhaled the mingled scents of medicinal chaparral and wet desert clinging to his clothing. He wore a dark-blue, cotton cowboy shirt beneath that sheepskin coat he'd hung up by the front door earlier. The Levi's he was wearing outlined the power of his long legs and narrow hips and made her lower body throb with need.

She had never gone to bed with Mark. In their high school days, they'd gone as far as kissing, but that was it. Mark had always held himself in tight check with her. That hadn't been Mattie's wish, but he was a man of lasting integrity and honor. He would never take her to bed before marrying her. In that way, Mark was old-fashioned. They had talked a lot about getting married when they were teenagers, but later she realized they'd been too young and innocent to do so. All they knew was that they always needed to be together, touching, and holding each other's hands all through their junior year in high school. Everyone smiled and called it "puppy love."

Mark poured himself some of the remaining coffee and took the pot back to the machine sitting on the counter. "You look good, Mattie. Teaching must agree with you." He sat down opposite her, sliding his large, calloused hands around the white mug.

"I'm doing okay," she admitted, giving him a half smile. "I like teaching English to Spanish-speaking children. They catch on so fast and are so eager to learn the language."

"You have a way with them, Mattie, because you make learning fun," he agreed, sipping his coffee. "You always did. I think you'd be a natural mom, too."

"I love all the kids I teach," she admitted, giving him a shy look. Mattie could actually visualize their children. Let's face it, there were many times she had imagined Mark and herself married with a brood of three or four children. The longings she normally found easy to suppress now surged through her body, and Mattie didn't know whether to weep, scream, or do both.

She had always known that Mark was the most frustrating person she'd ever met. She couldn't really blame him for his terrible childhood, or for running away from the ranch and joining the Marine Corps at eighteen. She would support anything he needed to do to escape Jeb's beatings.

But when he got out of the military and returned home, she had hoped they would resurrect the strong feelings they had shared in high school so they could share a future together.

It didn't turn out that way, however. Mark refused to stay at the family ranch and took a job with the Cavanaugh Ranch. The town's gossip machine flared for a week on his choice. Most people felt he should go back to his family ranch and help Sage run it. It seemed Mark always made decisions counter to what most normal people would have done and it continued to feed the machine that he was a dark person at best.

"Where are you going to live?" she asked him nervously.

"I don't know yet, Mattie. I'll drive over to talk with your Dad, Hank, tomorrow morning and see if he'll hire me to fill Pepe's position."

"Good. Did you know my dad just had his birthday yesterday? He'd love to see you. He always asks me if I've heard from you."

"I didn't realize it was Hank's birthday," he

muttered, frowning. "Darn it, I don't have any gift for him."

"Don't blame yourself, Mark. I'm sure Dad will understand. He'll probably consider you a gift." She smiled. "You're a part of our family, you know. My folks love you and Sage to this day. That's never going to change."

"Your family became our family, Mattie. I'll always have a warm spot in my dark heart for Hank, Daisy, and all you kids. You saved us in so many ways."

"You two were like an extra brother and sister to us. We loved having you with us all the time. We still do. You're our extended family and always have been."

Mouth tightening, he stared down at the table. "We wouldn't have survived without your parents' love and the four of you embracing us, Mattie." He shared a warm look with her. "You're a special family and you've always been there for us when we needed protection and love. You were the family we dreamed of, but didn't have. But you shared your dream with us."

Somber, she whispered, "You and Sage are loved by all of us, Mark. I know we're kind of a second family to you, but it was a loving one for you two."

"It sure was. When I was a Recon, Mattie, I was out in the boonies six months at a time. I've lost count of how many deployments I had. I didn't want to come into the firebase or where ever we were ordered to go in Afghanistan. I liked it out there. I didn't have to pretend to be social or watch guys who were. I had no family photos, no birthdays to remember, nothing to show off. No kids. No . . . nothing. I was always uncomfortable when the other Marines wanted me to come and look at videos on the computer, or photos sent to them from their wives or family at home."

"Hey, you were just trying to cope, Mark," she began.

Looking up, he held her sympathetic gaze. "Sage seems far more socialized than I am. I don't understand how she managed it."

"She's a woman," Mattie laughed. "Women are team players and networkers. Sage is very, very smart and she learned social skills because it helps her cope. That's why you and Sage spent more time with the four of us and our parents than you ever did over at your own ranch."

"Yeah, and it's a good thing Hank and Daisy practically adopted us. We were two abandoned, confused kids. Your parents didn't have to take us under their wings, and I appreciated it even as a kid."

"Hey, we loved having you two with us! We got into a lot of adventures and had a lot of fun together. You were our newfound brother and sister!"

He snorted. "Yeah, but we got into our share of trouble, too. Wyatt was always the shit disturber in the gang."

"And you were right there alongside him as I recall," she pointed out drily, grinning. "He loves you so much, Mark. And then, you saved his life in December. There's such a tight, wonderful bond between the two of you. He sees you as his brother, believe me."

Leaning against the chair, he gave her a searching look. "Funny how you remember the good times. All I remember are the bad times, Mattie. Maybe that's why I'm such a brutal pessimist."

"Oh, that was Sage's label for you," she murmured, shaking her head, "Not mine. You have a huge streak of kindness in you, Mark. I've always seen how you practiced with me and my family—and with animals and the elderly. So, I'm not buying into your 'dark' image. I know better."

Cocking his head, he held her lively, sparkling gaze. "Why do you always hold out hope for the hopeless, Mattie?"

"Because there's always hope, Mark. Just because you don't see it doesn't mean it's not there, just waiting for you to discover it. You got your hope beaten out of you by Jeb when you had no one to turn to, to protect you, after your mom died." Pursing her lips, her brows dipping, she added, "And honestly, I think if your mom had lived she'd have taken Jeb apart the first time he laid a hand on either of you."

"Yeah, Sage is a lot like our mother from what Jeb has said in the past. Neither of us remembers her, of course. I wish I did . . ."

"I can't conceive not having my mother in my life," Mattie admitted. "My mom Daisy is wonderful."

"Yeah, and your dad Hank never raised a hand against any of us, either. Not ever. Not like my old man."

"No, Jeb is a horrible human being and I'm sorry to say that because I ultimately believe every person is worth saving."

He stared at her, the silence deepening between them. "Mattie, one of the many things I like about you is your nonstop optimism. When we were growing up I believed in your idealism. But after Jeb started whipping me, I realized that your father was right."

"Oh?"

"I remember Hank talking one day, saying that there was evil out in the world. He and Wyatt were having a serious conversation when he was fourteen and I happened to be there to hear it. Hank was a Marine and he'd spent several deployments overseas."

"Dad doesn't speak often of his time in service," Mattie admitted in a subdued tone. "According to Wyatt, he was in the thick of the fighting over there." She shook her head. "I just can't imagine being in the military and having to shoot other people. I couldn't handle it." Giving him a glance, she added, "I don't know how you did it, either."

Shrugging, he said, "Hank had always said I was built for combat. That's one of the reasons I joined the Corps at eighteen. I wanted to follow in his footsteps, be like him. He was a man of honor and integrity. He knew what he was talking about and he always respected me. In a lot of ways, Mattie, he was the sort of father I never had but wished I did. He filled those shoes for me, whether he realized it or not."

"I know," she whispered, giving him a sad look. "As a kid I didn't really realize the extent of the hell that you and Sage were living with. But as I got older and saw your bruises and cuts, it made me realize not all parents were good ones."

"Jeb couldn't qualify to be called anything but fucked up, and he took it out on us. Or, he tried," he muttered darkly, brows drawing downward.

Wanting to get him off the painful topic, she said, "Call my dad tomorrow morning, okay? I know he'll be thrilled that you're back home for good."

"I will."

"Didn't the Cavenaugh Ranch have any openings for a wrangler, Mark?"

"I didn't even bother asking them yet, Mattie." He gave her a shrug. "I wanted to see you first. I know you know everyone in Van Horn, all the gossip and stuff. If there's a job around, I figured you'd know about it."

She laughed a little. "That's true, but when you care for children you always end up talking with the mothers, and then I get lots of information. We're the communications network here in Van Horn."

"I like that you never gossip, Mattie. It tells me a lot about your character. You never talk down to anyone and you always see the good in people."

Her smile dissolved. "I've always tried to live the Golden Rule, you know that."

"Yeah, Hank and Daisy drilled that one into all our heads," he said. "Treat others the way you'd like to be treated."

"Do you have a place to stay tonight, Mark?"

"I got a hotel room down at the end of town."

Mattie nodded, compressing her lips. "Are you going to continue popping in and out of my life without calling me first?"

He studied her across the table, hearing her censure but seeing something else in her eyes. "I came home to rectify a lot of things that were left loose, Mattie."

"Am I one of those loose strings, Reuss?"

Mattie asked, trying got keep her voice cool.

She received a quick grin.

"You know you've never been just a loose string in my life. You've always been my life line, Mattie."

"I just got an upgrade. Phew. Good to know."

Mark chuckled with her. It felt honest-to-God good to actually laugh once again. Mattie had always had that ability to lift him out of the darkness and shit in his own life. And now, she was doing it again. The sparkle in her eyes set off a gnawing yearning deep within him.

"You're the most important person in my life, Mattie, whether you realize it or not." He saw her suddenly become somber, staring at him, listening carefully to his confession.

"I know," he managed hoarsely, opening his hands, "that I haven't made you a priority. I pretty much ran out of your life at eighteen and abandoned you."

Mattie frowned and moved her fingertips along the rim of her cup. "Mark, you and Sage were abandoned by both your parents, but in different ways. I know enough psychology because of my teaching degree to understand why you did it."

"How so?"

"When a baby is abandoned at birth, it sets a pattern in him or her," Mattie explained. "Because you were neglected, you pass that behavior on to others without even thinking about it, without understanding the emotional pain it brings others. In this case, it hurts you and it hurts the others who are in your life."

"I'm a bad penny that keeps showing up in your life at odd times, Mattie, and I'm damned sorry I've hurt you. You're the last person who deserves that from me."

"But you didn't see your pattern," she pointed out gently. "For you, abandoning another person was normal."

"I see it now, Mattie. I really do."

"So when you said you're home for good, I believed it when you arrived here after your enlistment was up in the Marine Corps. But later, you suddenly took off again. You quit your wrangling job and you moved without explanation to El Paso." Her brows drifted downward, her voice lowering. "And now you're back. I can't help but wonder how long it will be until you suddenly up and abandon us again."

Pain drifted through Mark's chest. "I know I've hurt you, Sage, and my friends, Mattie. I never meant to. But something . . . came up five months ago. I had to go do it. And I can't tell you anything about it. I'm sorry." He held her gaze seeing the suffering in her eyes. "It wasn't planned, believe me. I did intend to stay here after leaving the Corps. I was saving money so someday I could put a down payment on a small house here in Van Horn. I had dreams for the first time in my life, but they got blown away by that job offer."

"I wish you could tell me what happened, Mark."

Hearing the pleading in her voice, he winced. "I can't, Mattie. I wish I could, but I can't."

"Wyatt thinks you were on some black-ops assignment."

He sat back in the chair. "I can neither confirm nor deny that, Mattie."

"Now you sound like my big brother," she muttered defiantly.

"I've come home, Mattie. For good. I know you don't believe it. But I'm out to prove it to you." He sat forward, elbows on the table, holding her petulant stare. "You have always been the most important part of my life, whether you knew it or not. Will you let me back into your life just one more time?"

# CHAPTER 5

WHEN MATTIE LOOKED into Mark's eyes, she felt a surge of hope. The dreamer in her wanted to shout, "Yes!" But the wounded woman who had often been left behind, was cautious. For a few minutes, she said nothing, absorbing his words and the energy between them, now crackling with tension.

At last, she spoke. Her voice was rough with emotion as she whispered, "How can I be sure you'll stick around this time, Mark?" He gave her a tired smile, recognizing the distance between them and the work he'd have to do to convince her of his intentions.

"Time will show you that, Mattie."

"But I'm afraid to reach out to you again, Mark," she admitted, honestly. "We had such big dreams in high school. A year before you left for the Marines, we were discussing marriage. And then you up and left Van Horn out of the blue without ever telling me why. I thought I was your other half, someone you trusted with your darkest, deepest secrets. But when it came right down to it, you left me out of any decisions. What was I to think about that?"

He dragged in a harsh breath, holding her shimmering gaze. "I was just too damned young and immature at the time, Mattie. It's not an excuse. I own what I chose to tell you then, and I admit that I was wrong. Believe me, no one's sorrier than I am that I mishandled the situation."

Mattie sat quietly, watching the play of emotions on his face.

"It wasn't until I was twenty-one that I saw how thoughtless I'd been where you were concerned. I guess I considered you as collateral damage in my messed-up life." He grimaced and looked away, frowning. Then, his voice shaking with regret, he added, "My hatred for Jeb spilled over into my attitude towards those around me, and that included you. I didn't abuse you physically, but I sure as hell hurt you emotionally. I actually abandoned you just like Jeb abandoned Sage and me. The difference was, he didn't want us—but I did want you."

Her eyes filled with tears as she sat before Mark and saw how agonizing it was for him to say these words to her.

"Look, the reason I left town at eighteen was

because I had to get away from Jeb or I was going to kill him. I had to get away before that day came. And believe me, it was coming."

Mattie's eyes widened as he continued opening his heart to her. It was as if he couldn't stop, once he began. "Mark, you never told me all this before."

"Hell, Mattie! I was so fed up with Jeb's beatings, the hatred was eating me alive. I even dreamed of killing him with my bare hands." He flexed his fist. "I couldn't take seeing him one more day, Mattie. It wasn't you who drove me off, it was my fear that I would kill him and be sent to prison to die. His life wasn't worth my freedom or my own life. So I left." He gave her a sorrowful look of apology.

"Then, you really didn't abandon me," she said thoughtfully. "You left because you were afraid you'd do something terrible to your father. Okay, I can understand that. I just wish you could have told me all of this at the time, Mark. Then, I could have seen your actions differently. You know I always had your back, even when we were two immature teenagers."

He pushed his fingers through his hair in an aggravated motion. "I've had a good ten years to think about what I did to you—to us. For the longest time, I've wanted to tell you all this. I did the best I could at eighteen, but obviously, it wasn't near good enough."

"When we were together, you never spoke of things like this, Mark. Why not?"

"Because being with you, Mattie, was like God's gift to me. I didn't have to be tense, on guard, watching for Jeb, or keeping him away from Sage. With you, I could relax. You made me happy. I needed what you gave me with your smile, your jokes, your laughter. You lightened my load, and I'm not sure you knew that, but I want you to know it now."

She stood up, pushing the chair back. "This is a lot to take in," she protested. "I sort of feel overwhelmed by it all, Mark."

"I guess I'm like a sinner going to confession," he muttered, giving her a tender look. "I've been carrying it around for a long, long time."

Her fingers tightened on the back of the chair as she stood there staring down at him. How fragile he looked. Mattie realized that he was trying his level best to be honest and vulnerable with her. That was a first. "I need time to feel my way through all of this, Mark."

"Yeah, I dumped a helluva lot on you tonight," he admitted sourly, standing and placing the chair beneath the table. "I didn't mean to drown you with it." He picked up his Stetson, ready to leave.

"It's okay. I just need time to let it filter through me. A lot of this I didn't know."

Cocking his head, he held her confused gaze.

"Take your time. There's been a lot of water under our bridge, Mattie. I'm sorry I never shared any of this with you before. You have no idea how many times I drafted letters and emails to you trying to explain why I did what I did. I wanted to tell you that you weren't the reason I ran away." He snorted softly. "I threw all my efforts away into the waste basket or deleted them because I do better if I can talk to you face-to-face."

"Okay," she said, trying to drag in a full breath of air, her heart pumping hard with shock. "Is that why you came here tonight? To confess all this?"

"I guess I did. I honestly wanted to thank you for tending my broken arm, to let you know I was better, and see how you were doing. I didn't mean to blather."

"It's all right."

He hesitated and then settled the Stetson on his head. "I'm going to call your dad when I get back to my hotel room and see if that job is still open. If it is, I'll drive out and see Hank about it. If not, I need to start scouring the area for a job of some sort."

He pulled out a pen and small pad of paper from his shirt pocket. Leaning down, he scribbled out some numbers. Straightening, he said, "That's my new cell number, Mattie. If and when you want to see me again, please call me, okay?"

Mattie knew just how much courage it took Mark to say that. He was leaving the ball in her court, not his. He was assuming that she wanted out of their relationship. But she could see in his eyes a small glimmer of hope that his choices hadn't completely killed their once powerful connection.

"I'll call you," she whispered. "I don't know when, Mark. I just need to process all of this, and it's not easy . . . you're not easy . . ."

"I know," he rasped. "I'll let myself out. Thanks for the great meal and pie. You've always taken care of me, Mattie, even when I didn't deserve it. Goodnight . . ."

*January 25*

MATTIE COULDN'T SLEEP worth a tinker's damn. She tossed and turned in her old, pink flannel granny gown. It was hardly glamorous, but it did keep her warm on a cold winter's night. Snuggled in her comfy queen-size bed, covered with a goose-down comforter, her mind raced back and forth over Mark's many admissions, trying to unearth what was beneath these revelations. Was this all simply an apology? Or something more?

Meanwhile, her heart was bouncing all over the place. First, she felt pure euphoria, then found herself plummeting into the depths of fear.

Mark had seemed so sincere. But his life had been one of undercover work, and she knew from what Wyatt had told her that he also had PTSD. Even her brother had it, so she had some inkling of how it played out.

Worse, Mark's hatred for his father was so profound that he'd actually thought of killing him! Mark had never indicated that he was capable of taking his father's life in all the years they'd shared together. That admission had been a shocker to her.

Maybe that was what bothered her the most—the fact that she really didn't know Mark as well as she'd thought she did. When it came to him sharing his darkest human emotions, he hadn't confided in her. That was what had hurt her so badly at eighteen, and now, finally, nearly eleven years later, he was finally telling her about them.

But it was too many years too late. Now, Mark was asking for a chance to get to know her again. But what did that mean? Was he talking about forging the same kind of friendship they'd had before? Or something more serious and intimate?

Her mind whirled with so many questions and no answers that it began to ache. Finally, Mattie got up around one a.m. and took two aspirin. She had to ask herself, What do I really want from Mark? Shuffling around in her sheepskin moccasins, she walked into the kitchen and poured herself a glass of water.

Turning, she rested her hips against the counter, grateful for the small, electric hurricane lamp in one corner of the living room. It shed just enough light to prevent her from bumping into a piece of furniture.

She stared sightlessly into the grayish cast of the living room. What did she want? Mark was so badly damaged that he could probably never change or get better at communicating with her. Could he? Would he become better at sharing with her the dead serious things that ate at him? Because Mattie needed that kind of openness and trust between them. Tonight he'd suddenly blindsided her with the truth and she was finding that it wasn't very comforting.

Right now she didn't trust Mark at all! Words were cheap. Actions spoke louder than words, and she knew it. But with all Mark's flaws, she loved him. That love had never been uprooted, despite his departures, his harsh childhood, and his secretiveness.

Mattie suspected the reason she had cycles of depression was because of her precarious relationship with him. She knew she had a tendency to stuff her darker emotions into a deep, dark hole. Maybe she was just as guilty of hiding her emotions as he was? And maybe? She needed to come clean herself.

★

*January 25*

MARK FOUND HANK Lockwood out in one of the big barns, opening up several bales of alfalfa in order to feed his brood mares in their large, roomy box stalls that were nearby. He'd called earlier and driven out at nine in the morning to meet with his friend, trying to tamp down the urgency he felt to get the job that was still available. Mark saw the fifty-one-year-old rancher straighten and walk down the concrete aisle way between the box stalls to where he stood.

"Hey," Hank boomed, grinning. "Welcome home, Mark!" He thrust his gloved hand forward, gripping Mark's.

"Thanks," Mark said. "You're doing real wrangler work, Hank."

"Yeah," he grunted, releasing his hand. "Pepe was indispensable. I miss the hell outta him, but I understand that he's gotta go home to take care of his ailing parents." He pushed the tan Stetson up on his short, brown hair peppered with silver. "I'm glad to see you coming home."

"It's where I'd rather be," he said.

"So you're staying home now, are you?"

"Yes."

Hank frowned and took off his gloves, stuffing them in the back pocket of his jeans. "I know you're a hard worker, Mark. And I know you could fill Pepe's boots around here. What I worry about is you suddenly leaving, like you did five months ago out of the blue. One day you were here, the next day you were gone." He draped his hands over his hips, his gray eyes narrowing on Mark. "I need someone I can count on all the time. I think you'll agree, you'd feel the same way."

Nodding, Mark said, "What I did five months ago wasn't something I expected to happen, Hank. It's not going to happen again." He saw the rancher scowl. Damn! He had always felt close to the man, because Hank had treated him like one of his sons.

"Why aren't you going back to your family ranch, Mark? Is it because Jeb's still there?"

"Yes. Sage has him compartmentalized, and she runs the ranch, but I can't bring myself to go over there, and I think you know why, Hank."

"Yeah. Sage has been doing a fine job of saving the ranch, no question. And she has a full complement of wranglers over there to help her out." He eyed him. "I'm sorry things are the way they are with you and Jeb."

Shrugging, Mark said, "Look, Hank, I have no aspirations about my family ranch. A few years ago I signed over my legal claim to it to Sage. She owns the ranch, lock, stock, and barrel. If and when Jeb finally dies, I won't go back there, either. Too many memories. No, Sage is the owner now."

He saw Hank's thick brows raise in surprise and pressed on. "Here's the thing. I'm home for good," he told him. "I want nothing to do with my family ranch. It's in good hands with Sage and I'm fine with that. I need to make my own way in life, and I'd really like to show you what I can do with Pepe's old job here at the Rocking L. I'll work hard, you know that. And I know the place better than most—I practically grew up on your ranch. You won't regret hiring me, I'll make sure of that."

Hank grunted and let his hands drop off his hips. "I've actually built a few houses for my employees since you left." He gestured toward the entranceway to the barn. "You can take Pepe's house—the one I assigned to him. I got rid of the bunkhouse a long time ago. It's the dark green house with white shutters, Mark. It's yours now. I'm not charging any rent, but you can pay the utilities out of your paycheck."

Relief coursed through Mark, and he broke into a wide smile. "That's more than fair," he said, holding out his hand to shake Hank's. "I swear you won't regret hiring me."

"I don't worry about your work ethic, son," Hank shook Mark's hand then clapped him gently on the shoulder. "I worry about you suddenly up and disappearing from our lives again."

Grimly, Mark said, "It's not happening again. There are a lot of reasons I want to be home."

"Is Mattie one of 'em?" Hank asked, giving him a thoughtful look.

"Yes."

"You two were closer than close growing up. Daisy and I always thought one day . . . well . . . that's a long time ago." He removed his hand from Mark's shoulder. "Get your gear and get settled in. Jake is our foreman now and you'll probably find him in our tractor and equipment barn. Go see him after you've moved things into that house. I'll let him know I'm hiring you."

For a moment, Mark found himself fighting back tears. He was so surprised he was temporarily speechless. Then, swallowing hard against his tightening throat, he rasped, "I'll do that. Thanks for giving me this chance, Hank. I won't let you or your family down."

Hank smiled a little. "You've always been a part of our family, Mark. You know that. Nothing's changed. You and Sage are like our children."

Relief avalanched through Mark. "God, it's been a rough ride," he admitted thickly, "but you and Daisy have always had our backs. You know how much that means to us."

Giving a short nod, Hank said, "We'll always have your backs, Mark. Now why don't you go get your gear and make yourself at home?"

What a welcome invitation! It felt as if the world had finally, after his twenty-nine years of hardscrabble life, given him an honest-to-God break. "I'll do that."

"Mattie know you're back, son?"

"I saw her last night, explained that I was back for good." He saw Hank's expression soften. It was no secret that he and Daisy had always thought they would marry someday. Mark wondered as he turned to leave, if they still expected that of them. As he walked to his silver pickup truck, he wasn't sure what would happen between them. He hadn't exactly been PC about a lot of things last night with her. And he'd tossed and turned all night, worried that what he'd shared with Mattie would scare her off. But he had to do it or he was going to lose her forever and he knew it.

Opening the truck door, he climbed in, the gray sky still threatening rain or snow. It was colder this morning than yesterday. As he started the Ford and backed out of the parking space near the ranch house, he had a sudden urge to call Mattie. But he didn't dare. He'd left it all in her hands as to whether or not she wanted contact with him again.

Even though joy threaded through him, there was a knot of fear, like a huge rock sitting in the pit of his stomach. He had so much to make up for with Mattie—so much. The woman he loved with all his life was the one he'd injured the most. His mouth tightening, he drove out to the highway, heading back to Van Horn and his hotel room where he had his life packed in a duffle bag.

Would Mattie call him? Or was she done with him once and for all? He had no one to blame but himself for his predicament with her and he knew it.

No one.

# CHAPTER 6

MATTIE MADE A point of having lunch with Sage at Spooner's Diner whenever she came into town to get supplies. Her hands were damp with nerves as she sat down in a brown, leather corner booth near the kitchen. It was always a treat to meet Sage—they were best friends forever. They had been incredibly close since childhood. Once a week, they came here for lunch and to catch up with one another's lives. Today, Mattie had some serious questions for Sage.

Sage had black hair with blue highlights, light gold-brown eyes, and was wearing typical ranch clothing. She always carried herself with pride, her shoulders squared beneath the sheepskin jacket she wore. Sage's foreman, an ex-Army Delta Force soldier, Jason Collier, had dropped her off and driven over to the feed store while she ate lunch with Mattie. Spotting Mattie, she raised her hand in hello and smiled warmly.

Sage removed her weathered, black Stetson and threaded her way through the many customers inside the popular diner. Many of them knew her, said hello and passed some pleasantries with her as she made her way to the corner booth. Sage, although very social, kept walls around herself like her brother. To anyone who didn't know the horrifying childhood that she'd survived, thanks to Mark, a person would find her kind and thoughtful. Mattie knew some of that was a "game face," as Mark called it. Inwardly, she was a lot more private and did not make many friends. Mattie was her only real friend in Van Horn.

It had been that way for a long time. Growing up, Sage hadn't known from one morning to the next if she'd wake up to see the sun rise. Jeb had made his children's lives an unending hell. They were like two frightened animals, terrified, always alert, and waiting for Jeb to disrupt their day—or night. It was no way for a child to live.

"Hi," Sage said, sliding into the booth, across the table from Mattie. She dropped her Stetson and purse next to her on the seat. "How are you doing?"

Mattie raised a brow. "I'm not sure, Sage. That's why I wanted to meet you here."

Sage smiled a little. "Let me guess," she said, taking the menu from the waitress. They both ordered coffee and after the woman left, she asked, "Mark?"

Nodding, Mattie quickly told Sage what had happened on December 24, when Mark had dropped in for an unexpected visit.

The waitress came back with their mugs of coffee, took their orders, and left.

"Have you seen or talked to Mark since he got back to Van Horn?" Mattie asked.

"Just yesterday. I knew he was in town because I heard gossip about it in the grocery store the other day. He's working for your dad now. Did you know that?"

Mattie nodded. "Yes, Mom called me two days ago and let me know Mark had been hired to replace Pepe."

"So you have a lot suddenly on your plate once again," Sage said.

"Yes."

"Are you scared, Mattie? Because you look like it."

"You always read me so well," she admitted. "I'm scared to hope again with Mark. He's left me twice. I can't handle it a third time."

Sage gave her a sympathetic look, sipping her coffee. "Yeah, I know that one. Because of my past, I'm afraid to reach out and love someone, too. I don't trust men, pure and simple. I want to, but Jeb's face seems to appear on every man who wants to get close to me. I thought as I grew older that I'd get over it, but I haven't."

"Jeb wounded both you and Mark so deeply," Mattie agreed softly.

"Which is why dealing with us," Sage went on, more matter-of-factly, "is a crap shoot at best. We're not a good bet for any kind of ongoing relationship. I've left a string of broken hearts behind me since high school."

Mattie nodded. She felt so badly for her friend.

"But at least Mark is close to you—he's always been that way. You two share something so rare, I really don't think I'll ever see it again in my lifetime."

"But even something that strong can be broken, Sage."

"Mark loves you and you know that. He fell for you in the first grade, Mattie. I know my big brother can be a royal pain in the ass and he doesn't always make the best decisions, but his heart has always been yours and that's never changed." She held up her hands. "I know what you're going to say, that too much time has passed and that Mark's made too many bad decisions that involved you. I get it, I really do. But he's not a mean person by nature, Mattie. He's a screwed up kid emotionally, and he's still trying to figure himself out at twenty-nine years old. Jeb did so much damage to him. The only thing Jeb couldn't do was destroy his feelings for you."

Mattie sat back, studying her friend. "Is that what Mark told you?"

Sage gave an abrupt laugh. "Hell, no! He's got so much he's hiding in the darkness, he never gives me a glimpse of it."

"Did you know he was close to killing Jeb?"

"He never confided it to me, but I could feel it around him, Mattie. I could see the hatred in Mark's eyes. I could literally feel him wanting to kill the no-good bastard."

"Did you ever want to?"

"No. He wasn't worth the consequences. Thanks to Mark, I was shielded enough to get through it. And when he had his stroke and became wheelchair bound, I felt freed forever. He could no longer hurt me. He couldn't stalk me, wait for me in some dark corner, and then try to rape me. Putting him in that small house a half mile away from our main ranch house gave me the room I needed away from Jeb, to feel free of his threat. For Mark, it was different. He was the one who took the brunt of his beatings, not me."

"Yes, and you beat an animal or human long enough, one day they'll turn on you," Mattie added quietly.

"I knew Mark was reaching that point. I could feel it. But he never gave it words, Mattie.

At least he has to you. He's finally given it voice, and for that, I'm grateful. I've found that sometimes just talking about the pain releases a little more of it from inside me." She smiled warmly, reaching over and touching Mattie's hand wrapped around her coffee mug. "You have been the most wonderful friend to me. You let me talk. You never interrupt me. And I don't know if I've ever told you this, but I'm so grateful you're such a positive light in my life. If I didn't have you to listen to me, I'm sure I wouldn't be where I am today. I'd still be stuck in my dark world, like Mark."

"That's his biggest problem, Sage. He won't talk about the deep, scary stuff. I thought maybe he was confiding in you."

Snorting, Sage said, "Mark has pushed down so much ugliness inside him, it's a wonder he didn't explode."

"Men are taught not to admit they have emotions, much less feel them or speak to someone else about them."

"True, and Mark's taken that to heart."

"I don't know what to do, Sage. I feel trapped."

"Because Mark wants to become a part of your life again?"

"I'm not sure yet, but he did indicate he wants something . . . some kind of connection with me again. He wasn't specific and I was afraid to ask."

Sage saw the waitress coming back with their hamburgers and French fries. "Here's our food," she said. "Let's talk after we've eaten."

Mattie nodded. In no time, they were enjoying the food and one another's company. After they had finished eating, Sage asked, "Why can't you start at the beginning and learn to be friends once more?"

"Because I sense Mark wants more—he didn't say that, exactly, and even if he had, I don't know if I have the courage to give him my heart again."

Nodding, she picked up a stray French fry. "Mark needs to learn how to honestly and fully open up and talk with you, Mattie. That's what is really needed here between both of you. You need to open up to him, too, Mattie."

"It sure would help a lot," she agreed, "but I'm such a coward, Sage. I'm afraid if I be honest with how I feel about him, it will scare him and he'll go away again." Picking up the ketchup bottle, she squeezed it across her pile of fries. "It would sure save me and him second guessing all the time if I was more forthcoming."

"So why not start there? Set the agenda. Tell him what you expect. If he doesn't produce it, you won't sacrifice your sanity again. He needs to be brought up short. But in all fairness, he's not a mind reader, Mattie. If he doesn't know what's important to you, you need to thread that needle with him. Otherwise, you're both bound to fail."

*February 1, Friday*

THE WINTER DAY was cold and windy as Mark rode his sorrel gelding, Tank, into the barn. It was nearly four p.m., and he'd finished his work for the week. Dismounting, he led Tank into the partially opened doors of the barn, taking him to the crossties in the passageway to unsaddle and brush him down.

The Lockwood family had invited him to have dinner with them at six tonight and he was looking forward to it. Would Mattie be present? It chafed at him, if he allowed it, that she hadn't called since their initial meeting. Un-cinching the saddle, he pulled it up and off the horse, taking it to the nearby tack room. The barn was relatively quiet, the horses having just been fed for the evening by another wrangler whose duty it was to care for them. The munching sounds, the soft snorts of the horses, soothed some of his anxiety.

While he loved Mattie, he had no idea how to go about fixing what he'd broken between them. It was on his list to call Sage and meet her off ranch property, maybe have lunch with her in town, or go to breakfast at Spooner's Diner. Tomorrow was Saturday and everyone had the day off at the Rocking L. And on Sundays, the Lockwood family always went to church and then had a late-afternoon dinner together.

This was the first invitation by Mattie's family to have him join them for dinner. He saw Cat and Jake, her brother and sister, all the time because they both worked on the ranch, too. They often toiled together on some major project that required two or three people. But since their last meeting, he'd never seen Mattie drive out to the ranch.

Cat had told him that during the week, Mattie didn't usually visit because of her teaching duties, but that sometimes, she'd join them for Friday-night dinner. However, she always joined them for family dinner on Sunday afternoons, without fail.

Mark wasn't about to ask to take part in the Lockwood Sunday dinner without an invite, even though he knew he was considered part of the family. He knew that he still had a lot to prove to Hank first. Knowing the rancher was concerned that he might up and leave without warning, Mark was desperate to show the rancher he was reliable.

"Hey, Mark . . ."

Mattie's voice drifted down the aisle as he lifted the thick, heavy blanket off his horse's back. He allowed the blanket to settle down on Tank once more as he saw her silhouette at the entrance to the barn.

"Hey, nice to see you," he called. "What are you doing out here?" His heart sped up. Mattie had her curly hair down, wearing a heavy, purple goose-down parka, pink knit gloves she'd probably made for herself, jeans, and sturdy work boots. The pink muffler around her neck only emphasized her flushed cheeks as she drew near.

"I'm here for Friday-night dinner," she said, halting on the other side of Tank, patting his neck. "How are you doing, Mark?"

Better now that you're here with me. But instead of admitting this to her, he lifted the blanket off and said, "Doing good. It's nice to be home again, Mattie."

"And back in the saddle," she said as she smiled at Tank, taking her gloves off and rubbing his ears, which he dearly loved.

"Yeah, I've missed throwing a leg over a good horse. I'll be right back, okay? Gotta get my grooming tack box."

Mattie stood there, loving up the gelding. She watched Mark take the blanket to the tack room and a moment later he returned with a small, wooden box in his leather-gloved hand.

"Dad says that you're a good addition to the ranch. I don't know if he's told you that or not." She smiled across the horse, meeting his gaze.

"Hank usually isn't very effusive with praise," Mark told her wryly. He pulled out a curry comb, quickly pulling it over the thicker muscling on the rump of the quarter horse, loosening the day's grit on Tank's skin. "But it's nice to know."

"Are you getting settled in? Do you like Pepe's home?"

"Yeah." He gave her a humored look. "Hank said I could repaint the rooms if I wanted to." He saw her eyes dance with laughter.

"Oh, you mean his electric yellow, red, blue, and orange rooms? Pepe is Latino. He loves bold, bright colors."

"Yeah," Mark said with a grin, "it's been tough to go to sleep in the bedroom with that bright-red color hanging around me."

"Have you gotten a chance to start painting the walls yet?" She pulled her fingers through Tank's reddish-colored mane, patting it back into place.

Shaking his head, he said, "Tomorrow, I plan to drive into Van Horn and buy a couple of gallons of paint. I figured this Sunday, I'll try to tone one or two of those rooms down."

"Want some help? I'm great at finding the right colors for a room, and I've been told I'm a pretty good painter." She paused, waiting for his response.

His heart leapt and he tried not to stare in shock at Mattie. She was winsome, girlish right now, not the somber woman he'd talked to that evening. Maybe Mattie had decided to accept his offer of closer ties between them. God, he hoped so.

She looked beautiful to him at this moment, and he forced himself not to stare at her like the voracious, needy male that he was. "Well . . . sure . . . I could use all the help I can get."

"Good. Ace Hardware has the best paint selection in town. I could meet you there Saturday morning, and we can pick out a paint that you like, go home and do a couple of rooms. On Sunday, I could drive over to your home around ten a.m. and help you paint the other two rooms. I might—if you're lucky—even bring a crock pot of beef stew for our lunch. Would that work for you?"

"I'd be a fool to turn that offer down!" He grinned, changing brushes for Tank's legs. Crouching down, one hand on the horse's front left knee, he said, "Can I get anything for that beef stew you're bringing us for lunch?"

"No. I'll make some home-baked rolls the night before and bring them along to go with it. I know you love your bread."

He found himself beginning to salivate. "I've really missed your cooking, Mattie," he admitted, smiling a little as he stood up. He saw her cheeks go a deeper pink and then saw her green eyes begin to sparkle. Could she be making a gesture of welcome to him? Probably not. Mark had discovered a long time ago that he was lousy at reading women in general unless they gave it voice.

"I was having visions of you in that bizarrely painted house, surviving on fast food," she teased.

"It's not that bad," he grinned. "But I'm still getting settled in," he admitted. Her happiness radiated towards him like life-giving sunlight, and even Tank had perked up. The horse loved her hands on him, his eyes going half closed. Mark wished that someday she would touch him like that. Was it just a dream that would never come true? His life had been filled with bitterness and challenges, not the sweetness of a happy family and a normal job.

"Mom called me a few days ago and said they were inviting you to family dinner with them tonight. She asked if I wanted to come and I said 'yes'."

There was a slight trepidation in her tone. Mark finished off grooming Tank. As he unsnapped the crossties from the horse's halter, he said, "Did you come because they asked you, Mattie?" He clipped on the nylon lead to the gelding's halter and stood there, holding her gaze. "Or did you come because you knew I'd be there?"

Mark knew that Mattie was fiercely loyal to her family. This was a family that lived, ate, and breathed together, unlike his own. Wanting to know if she was coming out of loyalty to her family or because he'd be at that dinner, was crucially important to Mark. He saw her eyes grow serious.

"I came because I love catching up with my family, but it also gave me a chance to see you again."

Mattie wasn't one to be political, so Mark took her answer at face value. The fact that she'd invited herself to help pick out paint and come to his home this weekend to help him repaint the rooms, spoke volumes, too. His heart did a hopeful flip-flop. "Good to know," he murmured, clucking to Tank, who followed him at his shoulder as he led him to his box stall.

Mark didn't betray his joy, but he felt like he was walking on air, not on a cold, concrete pathway. Was it possible that his life was going to finally turn around after all these years? As Mark slid the heavy oak door close and latched it, he was afraid to honestly hope that a new chapter in his life had just turned over.

But that look of warmth in Mattie's eyes had been reserved only for him. She seemed buoyant. Could it be she had made a decision about them?

His father had told him he was cursed. And he'd believed it. Could a curse be lifted, and was Mattie the one person who could give him absolution?

Some people were just dark beings, and maybe he was one of them. Mark wondered if other dark beings like himself ever craved the light? Did they want to shrug off the heaviness he always wore around his shoulders? Could he ever get that toxic mind chatter to shut down, once and for all, inside his head?

When he was around Mattie, his world changed one-hundred-eighty degrees from where he usually resided. She could lift him out of his mental prison and make him feel hope once more. She breathed new life into his fractured soul. She fed him with her smile, her laughter lifting him, and her optimism offering him a better way to see reality. If that wasn't love, what was it? Mark was pretty sure that it was. Because he'd never experienced these feelings with anyone else but her.

Hoping against hope, he took his grooming box back to the tack room, closed it up, and then walked out to where Mattie was standing, watching him. He liked the friendly look in her eyes—it made him feel good and strong.

"Ready to go for dinner?" he asked.

"Better believe it. I'm a starving cow brute."

He grinned at her as he walked by her side, leaving plenty of space between them. "That's one of the many things I always liked about you, Mattie. You ate food like you meant it. You enjoyed everything that passed your lips."

She cut him a wry glance as they stepped out

of the barn. She halted, allowing Mark to pull the huge, red door closed. "What? I'm not one of those women who eat salads all the time to stay skinny? Is that what you're talking about?"

He turned, a burning look in his eyes meant only for her. Mattie's entire body went from zero to a hundred in that split second. The thrill of Mark wanting her made her body ache for him. Then, the look was gone.

They walked down the gravel slope toward the ranch house on the other side of the pipe-fence corrals. "I know some women have a tough time keeping their weight at a certain level as they age, but you never have."

She laughed and said, "Oh, I have a large class of four and five year olds running around. You tend to lose a ton of weight that way!"

The corners of his mouth pulled upward and he drowned in her sweet, lilting laughter. "I guess you're right. It must be like chasing a bunch of calves down in a huge corral in order to vaccinate them."

Giving him a nod, she said, "Same thing. Only, in my case, the roundup lasts all day long!"

# CHAPTER 7

AFTER DINNER, THE Lockwood family offered Mark and Mattie some quality time alone. Daisy gently suggested a private place to chat—the family's card room on the other side of the house. "Why don't you take your coffee in there and relax a bit," she urged.

Mark was both relieved and nervous at the prospect of being alone with Mattie. Throughout dinner he'd sat opposite her, drowning in her country-girl beauty and wanting so badly to hear what her decision was regarding their on-again, off-again relationship.

At the dinner table, he'd forced himself to eat, even though his stomach was contracting with apprehension. Obviously, Mattie's mom wanted to put more meat on his bones, and he couldn't disappoint the woman who had been like a second mother to him.

Now, as he followed Mattie down to the card room, he wondered whether his whole world was going to blow up beneath him, or if Mattie was going to give him another chance. And he had no idea what she would decide.

Mattie opened the heavy oak door and they walked in.

Mark looked around the room. "You know, there are so many good memories in here," he said, shutting it quietly behind them.

"I agree," Mattie said, looking around the small room that had two card tables made of oak, bolted to the floor. There were four wooden chairs around each one. "Mom taught all of us so many great card games in here."

"I remember. Where would you like to sit, Mattie?"

"How about on the sofa?" She gestured over to the floral-print couch sitting against the southern wall of the room.

"Sounds good," he murmured. Mattie sat at one corner and Mark followed her lead, taking the other corner. He tried to read her expression, but it was closed, which was unlike her. He tried to relax, but couldn't, so he sat up, legs open, elbows resting on his knees, his hands clasped between them, holding her shadowy green gaze.

"When Mom called and asked me to come out for Friday-night dinner," Mattie began, her hands folded in her lap, "I was torn."

"Why?"

"Because she said she wanted to invite you to dinner, too." She sighed and gave him an exasperated look. "Ever since you came home, Mark, and came to see me that night, I've been up in the air about us. I'm just not sure what you want from me and what I'm willing to give or not give to you."

"If you want the whole truth, Mark, I'm scared, scared to try again with you. When you left for the Marine Corps, I was devastated! When Doug Freeman, who works at the local office-supply store, asked me to marry him two years after you left, I stupidly said 'yes'. I was still hurting because you'd left me, Mark. I was angry at you, and my heart was broken."

He said nothing, letting her find the right words.

"I married Doug, but eventually I realized I didn't love him. I divorced him when I was twenty-five." She drew in a ragged breath and pushed on. "That was three years ago. It hurt me as much as it did Doug, because he really, in his own way, loved me. But I wasn't honest enough with myself at that age to see that I'd rebounded from you with him. Doug paid the price for it and I'll always feel badly about that."

"I knew you'd married Doug because Daisy told me about it." He frowned and looked away for a moment, emotions swamping him. "I'm sorry for all the pain I've caused you and him . . ." He held her sad-looking gaze. "I saw Doug the other day in town. He's remarried now, and the father of a baby son."

Nodding, Mattie said, "Yes, he re-married a year and a half ago. He's happy with Rachel and I'm happy for them both. He absolutely dotes on his son, Randall. Things turned out well for him, despite what I'd done to him."

Shaking his head, Mark uttered, "I'm realizing that all of us make mistakes in our twenties, Mattie. I'm still learning what is and isn't right for us."

She studied him silently, then continued, "I just don't like hurting people. But—" and her voice trembled slightly, "I'd loved you for so long that it devastated me in ways I couldn't even begin to imagine before you walked out on me."

He saw her eyes fill with tears. "I just didn't know what I was doing back then, Mattie, and I'm so sorry. When I escaped from Jeb after high school graduation, I got the first taste of freedom I'd ever had. I had to get away from him or I was going to kill him. I told you that when I saw you back at the end of January."

"I know. I've had some time to go over our conversation in my head, and I talked to Sage about it, too. I needed someone else's perspective on us, Mark."

"You and Sage have always been like sisters," Mark said, watching her still struggling for the right words. There was confusion and bewilderment in her eyes, and he'd caused it all. Why couldn't he have made her happy and not been so damned selfish? Mark had no real answer. "You know, I never told Sage how I felt toward Jeb, either."

"I know, she told me that when we had lunch at Spooner's Diner. She said she'd felt it, but you two had never really discussed it."

"No, because to give it words would make me as evil as Jeb was," he growled. "I didn't want to turn into the same kind of bastard, but I was heading that way, Mattie. I had to escape Van Horn, the ranch, and most of all, Jeb. As it was, I ran off to the Marine Corps and used my killing rage in my black-ops work. And I killed plenty of the enemy. Each one had Jeb's face, in my mind and heart."

"Do you still want to kill Jeb?"

"No, not anymore. I worked out a lot of the poison inside me in the Corps, Mattie." He gave her a miserable look. "I won't forget any of the faces of the enemy I took out for as long as I live. That was when I realized killing Jeb would have haunted me until the day I died." His voice turned bitter and hard. "When I understood that, the last thing I wanted was to see his face every time I closed my eyes and tried to go to sleep."

"Maybe that's a good thing, then," Mattie said softly, giving him a sympathetic glance. "I'm just sorry that Child Protective Services didn't intervene."

"That's because Jeb told me that if I went to the sheriff and turned him in for beating me, he'd kill Sage."

Mattie gasped, her eyes growing wide. "No! He didn't really say that, did he, Mark?"

"Yes, he did," he rasped, "I was ten years old and I screamed at him during one of his beatings that I was going to turn him in to the sheriff. He grabbed me by my t-shirt, slammed me up against a wall, and told me that he'd kill my sister if I did—and I believed him. He was capable of it, you know that. There were beatings I took when I didn't think I'd live to see the end of it. Jeb had a killing rage in him that when triggered, made him lose control. I'm frankly surprised I actually survived him. I always felt like I would die at his hand someday."

Mattie sat up, her voice shaky. "Did Sage ever know about this, Mark?"

Shaking his head, he stared down at his tightly clasped hands between his thighs. "No. I never told her. He was stalking her relentlessly and I didn't want to add that to the pressure she was already under. So I took Jeb at his word and never turned him in. I was trying to protect her the best I could. Looking back on it now, realizing I was only ten years old, I didn't have the maturity or awareness I have now. I should have risked it and turned him in, but I didn't. Hindsight is always twenty-twenty."

Mattie suddenly stood up, hand across her mouth, staring down at Mark. "What a horrible position he put you in! You were the sole person who could save yourself and Sage, and you were muzzled by fear."

He stared up at her. "Jeb knew and I knew. That was enough."

She began to pace, wrapping her arms around her waist, her voice tight with tears. "Mom and Dad never knew about his threat either, did they?"

"No way. I knew your dad would turn Jeb in to the sheriff and I couldn't risk him killing Sage by telling Hank anything."

"But, Mark—" she whispered, shaken, "my whole family knew Jeb was abusive toward you. My dad wanted to get Child Protective Services involved to get you two out of there."

"I'm glad he didn't," Mark countered, "because Jeb would have found Sage and killed her. He didn't care about either of us. He hated having us underfoot. We were nothing but trouble for him."

Silence fell between them. Mattie stood there in front of him, sniffing and wiping tears from her eyes.

"I knew my parents wrestled with your situation, Mark. So often, my dad wanted to go over and talk to Jeb."

"Well, he actually did confront Jeb a number of times," Mark told her. "Maybe he never told you?"

"N-no."

"I was with Jeb at Charley Becker's feed store one day when Hank came in and cornered him. He told me to go sit at the counter because he needed to talk to Jeb alone. I did what I was told, and then I saw Hank push Jeb out the back door. I don't know what happened out there but when Jeb came back in, he was white with fear."

"Really? What did he say?"

"Nothing, but I figured it out later. For the next six months, Jeb didn't lay a hand on either of us. Hank probably threatened him, and it obviously made an impression on the bastard. At least for six months there was no more beatings for me. And he left Sage alone, as well."

"But then he started up again?"

The corners of his mouth flexed into a brutal line. "Yeah, gradually, Jeb went back to doing the same things to us. I almost went and told Hank about it, but I was afraid that if I did, he'd take it out on Sage . . . we had so many secrets, Mattie," he uttered wearily. "I'm glad that part of my life is over. I'm glad Jeb had that stroke. I'm just sorry it didn't finish off the miserable bastard. And I'm glad Sage owns the ranch now and that it's thriving under her care. At least, she's somewhat happy."

"What do you mean by that?"

"She's afraid to reach out and love someone, Mattie. Jeb wounded her so badly, she won't even give love a chance to grow in her heart and take hold with another man. It hurts to see how wounded she is—she's such a wonderful person. She does so much for the ranch workers, and she donates her time to the Delos charity in town, helping seniors make ends meet. Sage has never known love. But at least—" he held her gaze, "I know what love is. I felt it. I had it with you, Mattie."

She stood up and slowly circled the room. Finally, she came back and sat down, facing him. "Thanks for letting me know about Sage. It's just so sad. Jeb murdered a part of both of you." She looked away, gathered her thoughts, then turned and looked directly at Mark.

"What I told Sage was that what I wished for, more than anything else, was for you to honestly start communicating with me so I know what's on your mind and what you're feeling."

"Believe me, I heard you the last time we talked, Mattie. I'm trying to do exactly that right now with you." He hesitated. "But both Sage and I are so damaged that we can't always share light and happiness with you. All you'll ever hear about is the crappy childhood we survived. That's partly why I never talk about what I'm feeling. Who wants to hear it? No one cares. It was a long time ago."

"I care and don't you ever forget that. It's still alive in you both to this day," Mattie coaxed gently.

"Yeah, I realized in Afghanistan how I carried Jeb around with me like a dark cloud," he agreed bitterly. Pushing his fingers through his hair, he added, "I wish to hell I could do some kind of surgery to get those memories cut out of my head, Mattie, and make them all go away. But I still carry him around, just as Sage does, and that hurts me even more than I hurt for myself."

"Because you love Sage and she's your sister. You two went through a lot together—a war, a combat of another kind, really. And you bear the scars. Dad says that's what PTSD is all about: you experienced things that very few human beings have had to endure. It has to haunt you."

"That's why you were in my life. You never realized it, Mattie, but you fed my bleeding soul. Just your smile and the way your eyes glistened with life and joy helped me survive those eighteen years with Jeb. I never told you that until now, and I'm sorry as hell that I didn't do it before today."

"But you were caught up in a pattern of life-and-death, Mark. How could you?"

"You've got that right. To this day, I wake up and I'm grateful that even with all the blackness I carry inside me, I'm still glad to wake up and still be alive."

"Sage has always walked around what you've just shared with me, Mark. I know she's hurting too. I just wish . . . well . . . I wish she would know real love, too, like the tender love that I've always held for you."

"We shared puppy love, Mattie, but it was the single, most important joy I carried inside me. You were always my bright spot, my hope, my promise of a better future, together."

Nodding, she wiped her eyes and then pushed her damp palms down her slacks. "I want to start all over with you, Mark. I never stopped loving you and yes, it was puppy love. But I think that, for now, I need time before I can open my heart to you again. I have to see that you'll honestly share with me. I need to know who you are, beyond the secrets you carry inside. I want you to share ordinary, everyday thoughts with me, so I can be a true partner to you. I can't handle losing you again, Mark. It's asking too much of me."

He sat up now and said, "I figured that out since we last talked, Mattie. I've destroyed the feelings you had while we were growing up. Even puppy love was a good thing to be shared."

"I can understand a little better now why you

left that first time, Mark. I was assuming that you didn't really love me, and that what we had wasn't that important to you, or you wouldn't have gone." She shook her head, her voice ragged. "If only you had told me all of this before you left."

"I was in a bad state at that time," he said, sadness in his tone.

"I could have been a far better friend to Sage if I'd known."

"Secrets . . . so many of them, Mattie." Mark gave a doleful shake of his head and then held her stormy stare. "Are you willing to give us one more try if I work on staying open to you? Because I will try."

"Yes, I want to, Mark. But if you stop sharing, if you hole up inside yourself again, leaving me outside as you always have in the past, we're done for good."

"I'm going to do my best to earn your heart back, Mattie." He stood up, walking over to her, a few feet separating them. Seeing her hesitation, he didn't try to reach out to touch her. It was way too soon for that kind of intimacy. "Thank you for allowing me one more chance, Mattie. I know I don't deserve it, but you have such a big, wonderful heart. You'd forgive the devil himself."

Swallowing hard, Mattie whispered, "Mark, you remind me of a beaten dog, so afraid of everyone, afraid to being hit again. I get that.

What I'm really asking of you is to trust me. As a child you had no one you could trust except yourself, plus you were Sage's protector. An abused animal is always wary of others, but over time if it's shown love, trust can begin to build." She reached out, her fingertips grazing his stubbly jaw. "That's what I'm really needing from you—your trust."

His cheek tingled where she'd grazed it. How badly Mark wanted to sweep Mattie into his arms and kiss her senseless until she melted into him and they became one living, joyously beating heart to one another. Instead, he remained unmoving, his eyes narrowing upon hers. Her touch hadn't been sexual. It was caring, like the words she'd just spoken. He memorized the moment and the gesture.

Now, he was going to turn his combat experience into something positive and productive for both of them. He was going to remember each and every fleeting expression of Mattie's looks, voice, touch, and so much more. Mark was going to learn, one way or another, what it meant to sincerely love and trust another human being. He had no role model like a mother or a caring father to show him the way. But he'd do it, come hell or high water. He'd always loved Mattie, but it had been an innocent love. They were both older now, nearly thirty years old.

"Mattie, you're the most important person in

my life," he began, his voice thick with emotion. "I'm so far from perfect. I'm going to try and be what you need me to be, but I'm scared. Scared that I'll fail you again. That I won't read something accurately in you—or I won't see it. I'm afraid you won't give me the time I need to catch up in so many different ways."

She nodded and told him what he needed to hear. "I never stopped loving you, Mark. Not to this day. That's a long time, don't you think? I'm not going to set up a schedule or give you a drop-dead date you have to meet so I'll know if we're a fit or not. I would never do that to you. I know your past history and I'm not going to put a time limit or an unreasonable demand on what we're trying to do together. Does that help?"

Did it ever! His shoulders sagged with relief. "Yes, that helps a lot, Mattie. I just worry that I won't meet your expectations."

A corner of her mouth twitched. "None of us will ever fully meet the other's expectations, so get over that, okay? If I'm confused or concerned about something, I'll go directly to you."

"Fair enough," he murmured, giving her a slight nod. "I'll earn you back every single day, Mattie."

"We both have jobs, Mark. I won't be able to see you that often," she warned.

"Then we'll take what we can get and make the most of it when we do get together. All right?"

"Yes, that works for me."

How badly Mark wanted to enfold Mattie against him, hold her, feed her as she'd fed him for so many years. He saw longing in her eyes, and thought that she wanted the same thing as him, but Mark was afraid to trust what he saw. There was so much he didn't know about Mattie! How much he'd failed her in so many ways.

Standing a few feet away from her, inhaling her sweet feminine scent, watching the light above cast copper, gold, and crimson colors across her hair, he wanted to kiss her. But that had to wait. So did touching her intimately in any way. But he could at least reach out, slip her hand into his, which is what he did. Giving it a gentle squeeze, he saw her entire expression change to one of hope, one of pleasure. Sometimes, touch said more than words, and Mark understood as never before, this was one of those moments.

"Ready to leave?" he asked her, feeling her fingers curve warmly around his.

"Yes. You have a another long work day ahead of you tomorrow, getting those rooms painted."

He gave her a slight grin, led her to the door and opened it. Reluctantly, he released her hand and she stepped past him. "But you'll be helping me so it will be easier. Oh, and I'd like to take you to brunch at Spooner's Diner tomorrow morning before we go to the hardware store to pick out paint. What do you think?" He held his breath. Mark wanted to be with Mattie in a variety of situations. Would she like his idea?

"I'd love that. What time shall I meet you?"

His heart bloomed with unexpected joy. "Nine tomorrow morning? We'll have all afternoon to paint the rooms."

She smiled softly. "That sounds wonderful. I'll meet you at Spooner's at nine."

For a moment, he couldn't speak, emotions overwhelming him. "I'll see you then," he managed, his voice gruff and low. Maybe learning to show his feelings would be easier than he thought . . .

# CHAPTER 8

*February 8, Friday*

"THIS IS ESPECIALLY for you, Mark," Daisy Lockwood said, handing him a huge platter of fried chicken as he stood behind his chair. "I think this is one of your favorite meals, isn't it?" she announced proudly.

"Wow! This is great," he murmured, placing the platter in the center of the huge trestle table so everyone could have access to the golden bird. Friday-night dinners were a tradition at the Lockwood ranch—one he'd grown up with and loved. Ever since he and Mattie had gone to breakfast last Saturday at Spooner's Diner, his life had definitely improved.

Mattie gleefully told him that Daisy expected him to show up at Sunday dinners from now on also, and every time he thought of that invitation his eyes welled up with gratitude. It also confirmed that his lifestyle was changing for the better now that he had quit the DEA.

The group respectfully stood, waiting for Daisy to be seated.

"Daisy, thank you for inviting me to this special meal," he said, his voice thick with meaning. Hank nodded and pulled out the chair at one end of the table for his wife, and Daisy sat down, thanking him. She made a flourish with her hand, a signal for everyone to help bring the food in from the kitchen to the table and to sit down and eat. Hank ambled down to the other end of the table and took his seat.

Jake and Cat brought over two large bowls of steaming, fluffy mashed potatoes drizzled with rivers of melted butter, two bowls of steaming, golden chicken gravy, plus a large, rectangular casserole of sweet potatoes slathered with browned marshmallows and pecans sprinkled across the top of it.

Cat hurried back to the kitchen for one more item and pulled out the fluffy, lightly-browned homemade biscuits from the oven. She placed them in two large baskets and put one at each end of the table. Two jars of local honey were open and waiting to be used.

Mark had tried to help lay the food out, but everyone shooed him to sit at the table with Mattie, who sat opposite him. Heavenly smells were wafting into the dining room from the kitchen, and he instinctively breathed them in. Mark's mouth watered. It had been so long since he'd had so many home-cooked meals in the space of just a few weeks.

Cat and Jake traded jokes as they took their seats. Cat sat next to Mattie, and Jake sat on Mark's left.

"This all smells so great," he told everyone. "Thanks again for inviting me."

Daisy smiled as Mattie held out the platter of chicken so she could easily choose from it. Her eyes glittered with amusement. "We know you're making your home, Mark, but I figured you might be getting tired of your own cooking. And every Sunday, you are welcome to come and sup with us from now on. No excuses."

Grinning, he took the platter from Mattie, their fingertips brushing against one another. Hungrily, he absorbed their momentary contact. "You won't have to ask me twice, Miss Daisy." He had always called her by that name.

Once in a while, when he was much younger, he called her Mom, but as he grew older, he stopped. Holding the platter, he allowed Mattie and Cat to grab what they wanted. Then, he and Jake got their favorite parts of the chicken: the thighs and wings. Mark passed the platter on to Hank, seeing that there was plenty of white breast meat—the rancher's preference—left in it just for him.

"Well," Daisy murmured, spooning some mashed potatoes onto her plate, "it's nice to see you back with us, Mark. I just wish Sage could have made it over today. I know it was short notice for her."

"Maybe another time," Mark said. "She loves your cooking, you know. Just give her a week's notice next time because she's juggling a lot of things over at her ranch right now."

"She's underweight, and I think Sage is working herself to the bone because she can't afford another wrangler. And heaven knows, she desperately needs one."

His conscience smarted. If he hadn't hated Jeb so much, he would have easily filled that slot in order to help Sage.

"Now, honey," Hank counseled in his deep voice, "everyone is doing the best they can. Let's talk about only good things at this dinner table?"

Mark breathed a sigh of relief, silently thanking Hank, who glanced across the table at Mattie. She had arrived earlier wearing a pretty white blouse with ruffles around her throat. Her red hair was tamed and she'd clipped it with a tortoise shell comb her grandmother had given her. Tendrils still escaped, however, declaring their natural, curly independence. Tonight, she had worn dark-purple, wool slacks and brown leather shoes. He liked the handmade, knit scarf that she'd draped around her shoulders. It was white, purple, and pale pink with silver threads woven among the strands of yarn. Her cheeks were flushed, her forest-green eyes framed by those long, red lashes.

He couldn't help lusting after her as he sat her family's table. Mattie was so vital, so alive, exuding warming rays of sunshine from within her to everyone nearby.

"How did you like the colors Pepe used to paint the rooms?" Hank inquired lightly, a devilish grin hovering over his lips.

"It's a little bright. I felt as if I needed to wear a pair of sunglasses when I first moved my stuff in there," Mark admitted.

Cat and Jake laughed and nodded their heads sympathetically.

"That's okay, Dad," Mattie said, "Mark's letting me help him repaint those rooms. They're looking good actually, and we've just got a couple more rooms to go."

"Good thing," Jake said, his blue eyes dancing with mirth. "Pepe loved those wild, Latin colors."

Cat rolled her gray eyes. "Only someone from his mother's family would have approved. I can remember when we built those homes, that I'd asked him why he wanted those bright colors in his house."

Jake gave her an amused look. "Oh? And what did he say?"

"He said he wanted his home to reflect his mother's home when he was growing up."

Mark sobered. "And he's always been close to his family in Mexico."

"Yes," Hank agreed, cutting into a huge piece of chicken breast, "and that's why he left to go home. He's doing a son's duty and I respect him for that."

The table grew quiet for a moment, the clink of silverware against plates. Mark savored every delicious bite along with everyone else. When you grew up on a ranch, you never took food for granted. Ranchers lived close to the earth and they expected to work hard for it.

"What colors are you painting the rooms, Mark?" Daisy inquired.

"That was a problem for me," Mark replied. "I asked Mattie to help me choose some colors last Saturday because I'm not very good at that kind of thing."

"What man is?" Cat hooted, laughing. "Well, I'll give you this, Mark, you know who to ask."

Mattie gave him a warm, silent look across the table.

"She's much better at color combinations than I am," Mark said, drowning in the tenderness he saw burning in her eyes for him alone. It was such a damned intimate glance, even though it was at a family gathering. He had always loved that about Mattie. She made everyone feel special, as if each person was the center of her world for her. And right now, he was bathed in that green-eyed look that conveyed so much.

"So what colors did you choose?" Cat prodded Mattie.

Between bites of mashed potatoes and the thick, fragrant chicken gravy, Mattie told Mark, "Tell them what your favorite colors are."

Shyly, he admitted, "I liked sunset colors. Not bright, but the paler ones, if that makes any sense."

"It sure does. Pastels can give rooms a nice, peaceful feeling," Cat said with a dip of her head. "Good choice. Something pretty, but not blinding," she chuckled.

"That became our theme for choosing a color palette he was comfortable with," Mattie said wryly. "Tell them what your favorite sunset colors were, Mark?"

Shrugging, he said, "Pinks, golds, yellows, oranges, and the pale lavender you see sometimes along the western horizon at sunset."

Daisy waved her index finger in Mark's direction. "Young man, you're a lot more in tune with colors than you think."

He flushed, and saw Mattie's eyes mirror sympathy for him. She knew how much he hated being the focus of attention and why.

"I think you're right, Mom," Mattie said. "Matter of fact, I brought a bunch of color swatches from Marcia's Ace Hardware Store with me. I have them out in the glove compartment of my truck. After dinner I'll go get them and you can see which ones Mark chose. He's finished all but two of the rooms, and we've agreed to get together tomorrow to finish the rest of the painting."

Hank grinned, wiping his fingers on a yellow linen napkin. "Always organized—that's my Mattie."

Cat gave them a teasing look. "Mom's made pineapple upside-down cake especially for you, Mark."

"Sounds good to me," Mattie said, smiling.

Mark nodded, giving Daisy a grateful look. "You really did make a pineapple-upside down cake for me?"

"Yep," Daisy said with a big smile. "I told you: tonight's dinner was to commemorate your return to us, Mark. I wanted to celebrate by making your favorite foods—the ones I knew you loved as a kid here at our dinner table."

"Yeah," Hank intoned drily, "maybe that will keep you here and you won't run off again, son."

Mark winced inwardly, but kept his face carefully arranged. He knew Hank had taken a chance on him by hiring him as a wrangler. "There was a special reason I had to leave, Hank. It isn't going to happen again."

Hank grunted. "You have a home here with

us, Mark. You and Sage have always known that. You're nearly thirty years old, now. It's time you settled down and decided what you want out of life as a civilian instead of as a Marine."

"I've been giving it a lot of thought," Mark admitted, pushing his fork absently through the sweet potato casserole. He knew that there was probably gossip flying around town that he'd taken a wrangler's job at the ranch next door instead of going home to Jeb's place. Mark was sure many of the town's residents were judging him for that, but they hadn't been beaten half to death by Jeb, either. And no one except Mattie, knew the toll it had taken on his soul.

"I THINK MOM and Dad know that we're trying to patch things up," Mattie told Mark as they sat opposite each other at the card table. They were enjoying Daisy's homemade dessert, along with some fresh coffee.

"Your mom misses nothing. She never did." Mark gave her a kind look, wanting her to know it was meant as a compliment to Daisy.

Mattie shot him a humored look and was rewarded with a half-hearted smile.

"Yes, that's true. I went in to see Marcia at Ace Hardware mid-week about getting another can of paint and she asked me if we were an item again."

Heat rushed to her cheeks and Mattie lowered her lashes, looking at the huge piece of moist, pineapple upside-down cake in front of her. "I've had a couple of mothers asking the same thing."

"Gossip, good or bad, gets around here faster than a wildfire in Van Horn," he grumped.

Shrugging, Mattie said, "I told all of them that you'd just returned home and that we were still good friends."

"Did that explanation satisfy them?" he asked, cutting into a piece of the pineapple.

"Probably not," she laughed a little, "but it stopped the other thousand questions that were coming on its heels."

She traded a merry look with him. How the past few weeks had changed Mark! They weren't able to get together often, but when they did, she could see him actively trying to give her what she needed from him. That sent warmth trickling through her body, waking up her once-dormant heart.

Mark had been through so much. And now she was putting more stress on him of another kind. It didn't seem fair to Mattie, but she had no other way to get him to open up to her.

Groaning, he muttered, "We could do a box lunch in the canyon tomorrow after finishing those rooms. Do you mind if it gets back to our local fan club?"

Her lips curved. "Not in the least! I'd love a picnic after we're done painting those rooms. Do you want to ride to that canyon over on our property? There's a great stream on it."

"Yes, that was what I had in mind. Wyatt said it's one of your favorite places. I know it's winter, but it's supposed to be in the sixties midday, and no bad weather is coming through. I figured with your mom's help, I could pack us a halfway decent lunch."

"I'd like that. I just was grousing the other day that I'm not getting the exercise I need."

"What? Chasing those little kids around eight hours a day isn't enough exercise for you?"

Sitting up, Mattie met and held his warm, amused look. "That's different. I love to ride horses but I just don't get the time I used to when I lived here at the ranch." She patted her wool-clad thigh beneath the table. "I've completely lost my riding legs, Mark, so be warned— I'll probably ride like a greenhorn."

Snorting, he said, "That's highly doubtful, Mattie. Your favorite horse, Sugar, always likes being saddled up and ridden. She's a good mare with a nice, even disposition."

"Like me."

He grinned as he leaned across the table toward her. "Are you kidding? I would never compare you to a horse, Ms. Lockwood. Let's be clear about that."

She felt a deep blush appear on her cheeks. Mark brought that out in her. "Thank you for opening up to me," she began, catching and holding his glance. Pushing her fork around on the plate, she added, "I really appreciate what you're doing, Mark. In some ways, I feel bad because it's adding stress to you that you don't need. But I can see you're trying every time we come together."

He nodded, savoring the cake. "Thanks for letting me know. I guess I'm anxious whenever we meet. I feel like you're grading me every time we are together. I know that's not fair to you, Mattie."

"It's anxiety," she said. "And I'm not grading you. I'm always feeling anxious myself when we see one another. I want this to work out so badly, but I also realize I don't have full control over it. And I know you have good days and bad days with your PTSD symptoms, and that's in the mix as well."

"It's not easy," he agreed, "but you're worth the effort, Mattie. I'd like to be someone you look forward to being with, sharing time and space with—not dreading it, or feeling so anxious and stressed out that it's nothing but an uncomfortable place to be with me."

She gave him a sympathetic look and reached out, briefly touching his hand. "Hey, I've never felt that about you, Mark." Lifting her hand off his, she added, "I always look forward to seeing you. You make me feel good—happy. Didn't we have a lot of fun and laughs last weekend painting some of those rooms in your house?"

He grinned lopsidedly, cutting into the piece of pineapple across the cake. "We sure did."

"And didn't I suggest that we paint each room together, not have you in one room and me in another? I really enjoyed painting as a team."

"It felt good for me, too, Mattie."

"Are you okay with me coming over at nine a.m. tomorrow and we'll finish off those last two rooms? It shouldn't take that long."

He chuckled. "Yes, let's finish them off. Changing the topic, Mattie, I've never been as well fed as by you and Miss Daisy."

"Big surprise! Remember, I've looked into your refrigerator, Reuss, and all I saw there was junk food."

"I admit it—I'm not much of a cook, Mattie."

Mattie was already thinking about their upcoming paint session.

"One of the bedrooms will be a pale yellow and the last one, a pale lavender. Have you decided what to do with them?"

"Not yet. A three-bedroom house has more space than I'm used to living in, and I don't really have much to fill it up. The rooms are still pretty empty. Remember, the Marine Corps didn't encourage me to keep a lot of furniture and other stuff with me."

"You were on deployment all the time," Mattie said, frowning. "I asked my mom where you stayed and she said you lived in barracks on base."

"I lived there whether I was on deployment or not," he said.

"You've just had so little of real life to surround you," Mattie said, frowning as she finished off what was left of her piece of cake. Lifting her chin, she stared across the table at Mark. "Your life is like an blank canvas, and I understand why. Would you like me to show you some decorating tips to make your place cozier?"

"Yes, I'd like that a lot. Anything you can suggest will help." He frowned and then said slowly, "I don't know what it's like to live inside a real home, Mattie, except for your parent's home. I know Sage and I always loved hanging out here with you four kids, having lunch or dinner with you. It made all the difference in the world to us. Sage completely redesigned the main ranch house after I signed my portion of it over to her. She repainted the whole inside of it, too."

"I know. I helped her," Mattie replied, remaining serious. "It was so dark in there before. Now? It's light and airy."

"I'm not surprised that it has your touch.

There was no life in that house, before you helped Sage redesign it," he agreed, finishing his cake, and pushing the plate and fork aside. "A pretty sterile environment, looking back on it. Sage and I always loved coming over here. Your home was so alive compared to ours. It was warm and welcoming. I know when Sage took over the ranch, she had asked me how I felt about totally repainting the inside of our house. I told her to go ahead. I didn't care anyway. That place holds too many bad memories for me. I can go into a specific room and all I remember is the beltings that happened in it." He shook his head. "No, I was fine with Sage repainting it. I know there's a lot of family heirloom furniture and she wanted to hold on to that, and I was fine with whatever she wanted to do. I know Sage has memories of certain rooms in that house, too. I don't know how she handles it—because I sure can't."

"Well," Mattie whispered, her voice suddenly emotional, "you don't have to anymore, Mark. Why don't we look at your new house with fresh ideas? If you tell me what makes you feel at ease, we can add those elements. Your home should be a place you look forward to being in. I could help you redecorate the whole place if you want. I'd love to do that with you."

"Well, as soon as I get my feet under me, Mattie, I'd like that. Right now, the furniture in there is pretty heavy and dark wood. It reminds me of the house I grew up in."

"And it reminds you of everything that happened there, doesn't it?"

He pushed back from the table. "Yeah, it does."

"It's understandable. Look, Sage and I did a lot of antique hunting over half of Texas, looking for special pieces she wanted. It was a lot of fun."

To her surprise, Mark immediately responded, "Sounds like a great idea. Maybe we could do the same thing when you have time?"

She brightened. "Oh, I love antique shopping! Sure, we can figure something out with our weekend schedules."

"I just don't know what I want," he muttered.

"But you do know what you don't want, Mark. No heavy, dark-wood furniture. When I come over tomorrow to paint and go horseback riding, I'll bring some ideas along. See what you think, and if any of them call out to you, let me know. Okay?"

"Yeah, I'd like that, Mattie. God knows, when it comes to colors and decorating a house, I have absolutely no idea how to make a house a home."

She pushed back from the card table and said, "Well, today's your lucky day! I'm volunteering to be your own personal decorating consultant. I can't wait to get started filling up your nest."

Laughing a little, he walked to the door and opened it for her. "You always compare a home to a bird's nest, Mattie. Do you think you can make one out of mine?"

She halted a few feet away, the door opened. Looking up at him, she whispered, "I will make you a nest you'll never want to leave, Mark Reuss. You just wait and see!"

# CHAPTER 9

*February 9, Saturday*

"HAVE YOU MISSED not seeing your old house, the one you grew up in?" Mattie asked Mark. They had finished the painting early and by ten a.m., rode side by side, he on Tank, the sorrel gelding, and she on her favorite buckskin mare, Sugar. They were now in the canyon, a short distance away from the hidden stream surrounded by hardy trees that now stood bare in the winter sunshine.

"I never miss that ranch," he admitted quietly, catching her glance. "Not with Jeb still there. Most of my memories are of the Rocking L, and they're all good ones."

Mattie liked it when their stirrups touched from time to time, depending upon the swaying walk of the horses they rode. "I'm glad you have good memories, Mark. You sure deserved some."

He lifted his black Stetson off his head and then settled it back on. "You seem to be bringing them back to me, Mattie."

She considered asking him a question, and then decided to do it. Nervously, she asked, "Do you feel like you have a home, now?"

"Yes, and it feels damn good." They came upon the stream hidden in an alcove of bushes and wintering trees. Dismounting, Mark walked over and held Sugar's reins while Mattie climbed out of the saddle.

"Thanks," she said, smiling up at him. Mattie had wanted this Saturday ride and luncheon to be a celebration. It would join other recent get-togethers when they'd made some sweet, new memories. She took the reins over Sugar's head and led her over to the stream where the horse promptly planted her muzzle into the clear water. She drank deeply, and so did Tank, who stood next to Mark.

Mark looked and felt relaxed. Sometimes, Mattie saw him withdraw from her, but he wasn't that way now, and relief flooded through her.

"I love all the things we're doing together on these weekends," she murmured, coming up and sliding her gloved hand around his upper arm. "I've always wanted times like these for us—light, happy moments."

Reluctantly Mattie allowed her hand to slip from around his denim jacket. She could feel the hardness of Mark's muscles beneath the rough material, feeling them tighten when she slid her fingers around his arm. Her own yearning ratcheted up, wanting closeness with him as never before.

Mark cocked his head in her direction, meeting her upturned gaze. "There's nothing I want more, either." He smiled a little and added teasingly, "You're just a natural well-driller. You always see deeply into people's psyches and you dig for the real person. It's a gift, Mattie." She loved it when he complimented her. It made Mattie feel good.

"I know I ask a lot of questions—and you're right—I like getting to the bottom of things."

Now, she breathed in the faint scent of his sweat along with the soap he'd used earlier, a lime fragrance. Mark had shaved, as well. She was hungry for him, and had to stop herself from wrapping her arms around those broad shoulders of his, drawing him up against her and never letting go.

Her instincts told her Mark needed that kind of affection, too. It was something she'd sensed around him all her life, being abandoned early in life, that loss of nurturing, and it hadn't gone away to this day.

Mark looked over at her with deep affection. "Does it bother me that you ask questions or want happy times for us?

No," he rasped, turning toward her. He lifted his index finger and nudged a few strands away from her temple, holding her gaze. "You're a woman of incredible sensitivity. You care deeply and you don't take another person's plight lightly. There's not many people in my life I can point to and say that they tried to understand me and my situation. Pretty much, most of the time I get judged by others. But never by you."

Her skin tingled wildly where his gloved finger had barely grazed the curled, loose strands of her hair. Mattie's breath hitched momentarily as she framed that memory, his unexpected but welcome touch, and the soulful look of yearning she saw burning in Mark's gaze. How badly she wanted to sway forward, place her hands on his chest, lean upward and kiss that sculpted mouth of his. Reluctantly, she leashed herself, but the yearning continued to mount anyway. "I try to understand people's motivations, why they act the way they do. I guess I'm kind of an amateur psychologist—and believe it or not, I learn a lot just by working with my kids."

Tank lifted his head, water dribbling all over Mark's jacketed shoulder, and Mattie had to laugh at the sorrel gelding. "Slobber puss," she said, stepping away. Maybe it was fate that had intervened, because right or wrong, Mattie was going to take that step forward and kiss Mark. She knew she'd insisted on taking the slow road to reconnecting with Mark, but what she hadn't counted on was his natural male charisma, which had always drawn her close, and left her wanting more.

Leading Sugar over to a partly shaded area of trees, she took a pair of hobbles from the saddlebags and placed them around the mare's front pasterns. Easing the bridle off, Mattie left the halter on her, making sure the lead was looped in around the saddle horn so it allowed her reach down and nibble the dried, yellow grass.

Looking up, she saw that Mark was doing the same thing with Tank. These ranch horses knew the drill. They loved times like this, when they could take a mincing walk around and nibble on some winter grass.

Mattie enjoyed the warmth of the sun on her jacket, the heat stealing through it and keeping her toasty.

Mark opened up a worn wool blanket that he'd rolled up behind the cantle of his saddle and Mattie grinned, helping him spread it out after it landed on the grass. "Seems to me I remember this poor, ole blanket from our days as teenagers. I'll bet you do, too!"

He met her grin, walking back to the stuffed saddle bags. "Yes, I did. In fact, I asked your mom if she still had it, and sure enough, she did. She never gets rid of anything!"

Mattie laughed. "She's a pack rat, there's no doubt about that." She watched him pull out two, white plastic bags that contained their lunch. He had made their light meal with Daisy's help, but the fact he'd had a hand in it made her feel wonderful. She understood what she was up against: the fact that abused kids grew up to be self-centered and unable to relate to the needs of others. Mark had been that way with her most of the time, but now she was seeing him stretch, begin to grow, and put her needs first, not second.

Any child caught in the crosshairs of abuse for eighteen years was not going to understand selflessness. And in Mark's case, because he was always in the line of fire, the impact of such tension had changed the makeup of his brain. He was now in full-time survival mode. Mattie ached for him, loving him for putting himself out for her, and giving her new hope that they could make a life together.

The big question was, did Mark really know what she wanted? But she knew that would come with time. Mattie wasn't about to load him down with her dreams too soon in what would be a long journey. That guaranteed failure, and failure wasn't an option with Mattie. No way. Timing was everything and she had a world of patience because Mark was worth waiting for.

He walked over and halted at the edge of the

blanket, handing her one of the bags he was holding. "Lunch is in there. Daisy taught me how to make tuna sandwiches." He gave her a wry look. "Hey, it was my first time in a kitchen, so don't be too hard on me, okay?"

She felt his concern and knew how much he wanted to please her. "There's a first time for everything. And I'm not worried. My mom's a pretty good teacher." She took the bag, their fingers touching briefly.

Settling down on his knees, Mark took off his Stetson and laid it in a nearby corner. "Yup. She was kind, as always, and patient, for sure, with the likes of me."

His voice sounded wistful and she understood why. "When my head could reach the counter, that's when Mom started getting me involved in learning to cook." Mattie opened the bag. Inside were two Ziplocs containing plump, tuna-fish sandwiches on what looked like her mother's homemade twelve-grain bread.

"These look great, Mark!" She handed one to him and took the other. There was also a bag of Fritos and with a small jar of sweet pickles inside the other plastic bag. "You got me my Fritos!" Mattie crowed with delight, her smile deepening. She wanted to do everything she could to make Mark feel good about his first attempt to make a meal.

Mark avoided her eyes. "Well, I know how

much you've always loved them," he murmured. He opened the plastic and pulled out the sandwich.

The little boy who resided in him was still very wounded and unloved. Now, Mark's shyness touched Mattie as nothing else could. "Thank you . . . for making this lunch. It was so thoughtful of you."

With a slight, shy shrug, he bit into his sandwich, his gaze fastened on the blanket.

She realized he was having difficulty taking her compliment. To change the energy between them, Mattie took a handful of Fritos and placed them on the plastic bag, nudging it in his direction. She knew Mark liked them, too.

"You know, for your first foray into a kitchen, you've outdone yourself. I love the sliced almonds you mixed into the tuna salad. That has to be your idea because Mom never puts them in."

"It was, sorta," he admitted hesitantly, picking up a few Fritos.

"Did Mom taste your mix after you made it?"

"Yes, she did."

"What did she think of the addition of the almonds?"

"She liked it. I was surprised."

"Why?"

"I don't know. I just was." Again, the unsure and shy child was speaking, not the man.

Munching on the Fritos, she held his dark gaze. "You just need to hang out with people who appreciate you, Mark. They'll support you one-hundred percent, and they will never make fun of your efforts to better yourself."

She suddenly remembered when Mark had been bullied in second grade. Mattie had seen it with her own eyes, and had told her parents how three bigger boys were beating up Mark nearly every day.

Her father was getting ready to go to the school and notify the administration when Mark decided he'd taken enough beatings. The next time they attacked him, instead of trying to run, he stood his ground and fought back. The bullies were so surprised by the skinny kid who was inches shorter than they were, giving them each a bloody nose. They never went after Mark again.

"I've been thinking along those lines," Mark said, finishing off the first half of his sandwich and reaching for the other half still in the bag. "I've tried to use something you told me just before I left you last time, Mattie."

"Oh? What did you remember me saying?" She often wondered how much he'd taken in of her ideas, so this was a surprise.

"That we're all caught in our own family patterns and that mine wasn't of my making. We were having a talk about parents at the time when you mentioned it. I really took that to heart,

Mattie, and I began to see what you already saw."

"I give you so much credit for remembering that. Good for you."

"I know I gave you a doubtful look at the time when you were sharing with me, but it stuck with me, Mattie. You should know that it's helped me so much since then."

Tilting her head, she studied him in the lulling quiet. "Which part stuck?" She saw his eyes gleam with amusement at her question.

"The pattern of abuse. It caught my attention. I started reading some books on it after that, Mattie, but I got pulled away on this other job before I could dive into it fully. I still have the books and I intend to finish them and learn from them."

They ate in companionable silence. Mattie knew better than to insist that Mark tell her what was going on inside him right now. But they were definitely making progress. They finished the sandwiches and put the chips and pickles back into the plastic bags. He set them aside and Mark brought over another plastic sack from one of the saddle bags.

"Now," he said, holding her gaze, "this is my first stab at making dessert. I asked Miss Daisy if she'd teach me how to make chocolate-chip cookies. I know they're a favorite of yours, Mattie. I wanted something special for us today."

Touched, she whispered, "It's already been

special, Mark. But I can't wait to taste them."

He pulled out a square plastic box. "Here, these are for you . . ."

Their fingers met and Mattie cupped his hands in hers, holding them, seeing his surprised reaction. "Mark, you are a hero to me. You have such a good heart." She squeezed his hands gently and then took the box of cookies.

"It's my first attempt, so don't expect them to be perfect," he warned.

She eagerly opened the plastic lid and looked inside the container. They looked wonderful. "You can't mess up cookies, Reuss. It's impossible."

Mattie saw about half a dozen cookies that had broken apart by the ride out to the canyon. "I don't see anything here that will stop me from diving into these," she said, and popped a few chunks into her mouth, chewing slowly. Then, a look of pleasure crossed her features.

"I don't know . . . they look pretty beat up to me," he muttered, scowling down at the chunks and crumbs. "I was hoping they'd keep their shape and look like real cookies."

She laughed and said firmly, "Where they're going, Mark, appearance is the last thing I'm looking for. It's all about taste, right?" She saw a slight hitch come to one corner of his mouth over her teasing, and then proclaimed, "These taste great!" and she reached for more.

Mark looked relieved as she continued wolfing down the broken cookie bits. Then, he slowly reached over and took a few of the larger chunks. Popping them into his mouth, he chewed on them.

"They're really good, aren't they?" Mattie said, a big smile on her face.

"Yeah," he mumbled, "they're not bad . . ."

"Well, don't look so surprised, Reuss. Like I said, you can't mess up a cookie!" She grabbed several more fragments of cookie and saw his shoulders, which had been taut, relax.

Now, Mattie knew why he'd been tense during lunch: Mark was worried the cookies would taste bad even if his tuna efforts were a success. How many times had Jeb criticized him? Probably too many to count, which explained his demeanor right now. Was he expecting her to tear into him? Tell him he was no good at doing anything like Jeb always had? Mattie would never do that to him—or to anyone else.

To her relief, she watched a boyish grin broaden across his face. At last, he believed her, and was accepting her praise. He'd heard all his life he was no good, that he wouldn't amount to anything, and that he couldn't do anything right. Now, he was learning that he could succeed at something, and it filled her with pride.

After they picked through the cookies, nothing but some tiny crumbs were left at the bottom of the plastic box. Mark picked it up, snapped the lid back on, and slid it into the plastic bag. Leaning over, he opened the thermos and produced two heavy mugs.

"Coffee to go with our cookies," he teased, pouring her a cup.

"Thanks, this is the perfect feast, Mark. I'm full, my tummy is happy, and my taste buds are singing." She saw a rare sparkle, in his eyes as he allowed himself to lap up her genuine praise.

"I'm glad." He set his red plastic mug aside, capped the thermos, and set it near the bags. Picking up his coffee mug again, he cradled the cup in both hands between his crossed legs. "Mattie, there's something I want to discuss with you," he began heavily, his brows pinched. "I think you need to know about it."

"Okay," she said, hearing the seriousness in his voice, the apprehension and low tone of it. "Mark, I'm here for you. I always have been. Whatever it is, we'll deal with it together."

He was quiet a moment, then began, "No one has been more loyal, true, and honest with me than you have, Mattie." He moved his hands around the cup, staring down at it for a moment, trying to gather the words he wanted to say. Heaving a ragged sigh, he forced himself to hold her gaze. "And I trust you more than anyone on this earth. You know that, don't you?"

"Yes, I do, Mark."

"Well," he muttered, "I have something so top secret, so damned dangerous, that if it got into the wrong hands, it could become deadly. But I need to share it with you, anyway. Because if I don't, I'm afraid I'll lose you. And I've lost everything else in my life. You've been the only one to stand by me come hell or high water. You've defended me. You've always cared for me, like a mama bear with her cub."

Shaken by the tone in his tightening voice, the utter bleakness in his expression, Mattie felt fear race through her. When Mark said, "top secret," what did that really mean? Was he going to tell her something from his past as a Marine? "Mark, just tell me, please. What on earth is going on?"

# CHAPTER 10

MARK TRIED TO gird himself for what he was about to share with Mattie. His gut was as tight as a rock, his pulse skyrocketing, adrenaline starting to leak into his bloodstream.

Mattie sat there, trying to convey calm despite the fears that began to rise within her. She was determined to give him all the support he needed.

Mark looked up at her and felt so much damned love for her that he could barely admit it to himself. He knew he had to get this out in the open because if he didn't, he'd lose her. It was an instinctive knowing that had saved his life, and Mark always paid attention to it.

"What I'm going to say can never be repeated to anyone, Mattie, not even Wyatt. I know how close you are to your brother, but he's in the security business at the highest levels. I love him like he was the brother I never had, but he can't know of this conversation. Do you promise?" He drilled her with a hard look to emphasize how important this was to them both. Mark could see her wrestling with his request.

"Is this about something illegal?" she asked, finally. "Because if it is, maybe you'd better not tell me, Mark."

He knew the gossip around town the last several months was that he'd gone into the drug trade as a drug soldier. There was nothing he could do to stop that kind of talk, but he could see Mattie knew about it. "This isn't illegal. It's top secret."

"Okay . . ." she whispered, rubbing her brow.

"I hope you know better than to listen to gossip, Mattie."

She snorted a little. "Ever since you suddenly disappeared and someone saw you driving a truck with a Mexican license plate across the US border at El Paso and into Ciudad Juarez the word was out. You were tagged a drug runner," she winced. "And worse."

He shook his head, looking uncomfortable, but not guilty. "I know there's gossip from some of the town folk that I'm a no-good drug runner."

"Well, I never believed it!" Mattie declared strongly, straightening, her fists clenching momentarily. "You warned us before the

Cardona cartel came across our property that night just before Christmas. You saved Wyatt's life, too." Her voice broke. "Mark, whatever you were doing, you came through for us that night. That's all that matters to me." She pressed her hand against her heart. "You proved you were on the right side of the law. You saved my brother, and I don't need to know anything else."

"I know you don't think I'm a bad guy."

She stared hard at him. "Then what are you going to tell me? Does it have something to do with that night?"

He squirmed again. Mattie's unerring intuition had hit the mark. "Yeah," was the clipped reply. "Yeah, it's part of it, but not the whole story. But after I tell all of it to you, Mattie, you can never speak of it again to anyone but me. If you do, you can put us and both our families at risk."

She blanched, her mouth tightening. "I promise to tell no one. Go on . . ." she told him.

"When I was in the Marine Recons, one of my best friends, a buddy in my unit, was Sergeant Juan Martinez. We saved each other's hides so many times in Afghanistan that I lost count. Juan was happily married to Maria. They had a home in Nogales, Arizona. Paloma, their baby daughter, had just been born when Juan and I got assigned to the recon unit over there."

He looked around as if to assure himself no

one was nearby, then returned his attention to Mattie, who sat tensely, hands tightly clasped. "We were together in that same unit for five years, Mattie. Juan became like a brother to me, just as Wyatt is. He got out when his enlistment was up two years ago and I lost track of him. He just seemed to have disappeared off the face of the earth. I tried to get hold of Maria by Skype and email, but she'd disappeared, too."

"That seems odd . . ." Mattie murmured. "Good friends usually keep in touch."

"Yeah," he said, heaving a raspy sigh. "It was totally unlike them. When I wasn't on deployment, I was at their home in Nogales, Arizona, sleeping on their couch. We were all very close, and little Paloma always remembered me when I showed up. I came home, once a year for thirty days of leave, and they asked me to stay with them. So, yes, it was upsetting to me to lose track of them. Something didn't feel right."

Mattie nodded. She was feeling concern about Mark's friends, too.

"When my enlistment finished, I went straight to Nogales to look up Maria, hoping to find Juan and find out what was going on with them. The house they had bought was no longer theirs—it had been sold and someone else was living there. The new owners didn't know where Juan and Maria had gone. Then, when I was at a family kind of joint called Dollar Diner over in

Rio Rico, on the way back north from their place, I got a call on my cell from the DEA four months after coming home. They wanted me to stop in Tucson and talk to the regional director. They had a job offer for me."

"The DEA?" she muttered, scowling. "The Drug Enforcement Administration?"

"Yes . . . of course I did as they asked and stopped by the federal building in Tucson. The director wanted to hire me for a special under-cover assignment. He told me that Juan Martinez had been a DEA undercover agent since he'd left the Marine Corps. He was working his way up through the Cardona cartel in Chihuahua, Mexico. The DEA wanted to capture Diego Cardona, their leader, by luring him across the US border. It was Juan's job to figure out Diego's comings and goings, and he'd spent two years insinuating himself into the cartel."

"Uh, oh. Something happened, didn't it?"

"Yes." His voice grew tighter, and Mark was clearly fighting back his emotions. "One of Cardona's men didn't trust Juan. No one knew why. But Juan received intel that they were going to set him up and kill him. He found out the details of the plan from one of his cartel buddies who didn't want to see him taken out. The plan was to take Juan across the border to the US and shoot him in the head, placing his body in the vehicle and burning it so he'd never be identified."

"Oh . . . no!" Mattie cried. "How horrible!"

"When the director told me that, I knew I'd take his assignment. The DEA wanted me to go directly to Cardona's headquarters and try to get hired by them. They gave me a fake name and a fake history that would be verifiable when the cartel checked me out. I grew a beard so they wouldn't know what I looked like without one. It was just part of my cover."

Her eyes widened. "Did Juan know about this?"

"Eventually, when he saw me show up, he knew something was up. Of course, I wasn't at all sure I could pull off what the DEA wanted. They were trying to save Juan and his family. To do that, I'd have to be adopted by the cartel and accept a challenge from the drug lord to test my loyalty."

"What does that mean?" Mattie asked.

"Every drug soldier has to go out and kill someone Diego wants murdered. If the soldier refuses, he's shot by a loyal soldier in the head and disposed of. The DEA wanted me to offer to take Juan across the border as proof of my loyalty to the drug lord of the cartel."

Grimacing, Mattie stared at him for a long moment. "You weren't really going to kill him, were you?"

"No. But nearly three months into my undercover assignment, I overheard Diego talking to his lieutenants. They decided that they wanted Juan's body found in the US, somewhere in Arizona, knowing he was an American citizen. They decided to get Juan transferred to the US under some phony order, where they'd kill him, keeping Cardona's hands clean in his home country. They would stage the murder far from the El Paso border area and have it occur in Arizona. That way, they were hoping authorities in the US would think it was a robbery gone bad."

Mattie sat taking this all in. Who would have suspected what Mark had gone through, when others were thinking he was a drug runner? He was a hero!

Mark went on, not looking at Mattie, his thoughts back in the past he was describing. "Cardona didn't want to lead law enforcement back to Mexico, or to kick up the DEA's interest in his Mexican operations in Texas. He was afraid there would be issues with his shipments across the border to the US. They wanted Juan killed quietly in Arizona and leave no trace of their involvement."

"Why wouldn't Cardona make you kill someone earlier than three months?"

"Because I became his personal driver. I wasn't out doing drug trafficking runs. Diego took a liking to me, and I don't know why. But when I went to talk to him and ask for a job, he said he needed a driver more than he needed another drug soldier. His other driver, Oscar, had just been killed in a shootout with a rival Mexican cartel that was trying to take over some of Diego's turf in the Sonora region. I told him I was a damned good driver and a mechanic. He took me at my word and I was hired."

"That was lucky," Mattie breathed.

"Everything about an undercover assignment is dicey, Mattie. Yes, I got lucky."

"But what about Juan? Was he there at HQ, too?"

"Yes, but in a different capacity. He was a drug soldier. He drove one of the four trucks that carried marijuana, packages of cocaine, and pharmaceutical drugs to Diego's headquarters from different parts of Mexico."

"When he saw you, what did he do?"

"Nothing. He kept his game face on just like I did."

"Did you ever get a chance to talk with him alone, away from Cardona and his men?"

"Yes, about three weeks into my assignment, we had an opportunity and took it. Then, I told Juan everything. He was relieved but he, like me, knew the DEA mission I'd volunteered for had less than a fifty-percent chance of success. Juan was more worried about Maria and Paloma being murdered, than about himself. I told him the

DEA had already whisked them into the Witness Protection Program so they couldn't be found and killed. He was relieved to know if we pulled this off, he would be immediately reunited with his family."

She gave him a worried look. "You all had such terrible stress to deal with! Did Maria know what was going on?"

"She was told Juan was in trouble, but the agency didn't go into the details with her because the less she knew, the better. The DEA had agents come to her home and tell her that if she didn't sell the house and come with them, Diego would order his drug soldiers to murder her and her daughter. She willingly went into WITSEC, the US Witness Security Program. They're now safe."

Rubbing her brow, she whispered, "My God, Mark, this is so dangerous—for all of you!"

"I went in knowing that I might not make it out, Mattie. I knew I had to try because these people are like family to me. They've always had my back, always cared for me, and now I wanted to return the favor."

"How did you do it? I mean, this seems like such a risky situation."

"All undercover work is," he said grimly. "If I hadn't been a Recon behind the lines, as well as having worked in black ops, I don't think I could have pulled this off."

"What happened?"

"In the end, I persuaded Diego to let me prove my "manhood" and loyalty to him by taking Juan across the border, near Nogales, Arizona, to kill him. He was very pleased with the idea and gave me permission. Juan was hand-cuffed and I drove him across the border one night in an old, rusted Ford pickup truck. I had no one else with me, but Cardona wanted a video of Juan's body in the truck I drove when I returned to his HQ. I told him I'd get it."

"So you both escaped?"

"Well, the DEA met us at a pre-arranged spot on American soil that night. They had a male cadaver with them and we put it in the truck, threw on the gasoline and burned him and the truck while I took the video. They immediate-ly took Juan back to Tucson. I headed back to Cardona with the proof because it was important he think Juan was dead. We didn't want that cartel to think otherwise or they'd try and find him and kill him and his family.

I took the video to Cardona and he was pleased, congratulated me and now I was a full fledged member of his 'family.' At the same time? I knew of the semi-trucks that were going to come across Wyatt's ranch a week after that, so I stayed around to take part in it. I was able to contact the DEA and notify them. I then wanted to warn Wyatt through you, Mattie, which is why

I came up for that visit just before Christmas, to warn you. Except, Tal Culver was there and cut it short.

I pivoted, told you to tell Wyatt and left, going back over the border to wait for the mission to take place two days later. It was the best I could do to warn your family ahead of time."

Mattie shook her head, "This is so complex, and so dangerous for you, Mark. You're incredibly brave."

"I decided that night after the government agencies stopped Cardona's trucks on that dirt road on Lockwood ranch property, that I wasn't going back to Cardona. I was finished. Seeing Wyatt almost die of a heart attack did something to me, Mattie. I just wanted out of this business of killing all together. That's when I came to you to help me with my broken arm, and you did. I holed up in a warehouse about a mile from where you lived. My handler called the next day, and they sent a car from El Paso to come and pick me up. I quit the DEA and I came home to you. To a life I wanted more than anything else."

Mattie stared in disbelief at him. "Oh, Mark, that was such a dangerous operation to undertake!"

Shrugging, he asked, "What in life isn't?"

"So Juan and his family now have new names and identities?"

"Yes. Even I don't know where they're at

and I don't want to know. They deserve to have a permanent safety net so they can go on and lead normal lives. Juan served his country in the military, and then he joined the DEA after his service, and again, sacrificed himself and his family. I'm glad the DEA had his back and supported him when everything went to hell in a hand basket."

"But you sacrificed, too, Mark."

"I would do this mission in a heartbeat all over again if I had to, Mattie. I love that man like a brother. I always will. Love doesn't die or stop just because things get rough and challenging."

She compressed her lips. "I'm so proud of you, Mark."

"You know, I take care of the people who are important to me, Mattie. I'd go to hell and back for them. That's why I came to your kindergarten class, to warn you that Cardona was going to drive across Rocking L land."

"And no one knows what you've done to help so many others," she rattled, tears coming to her eyes. "If they only knew . . ."

He reached out, his hand covering hers for a moment. "Mattie, what they think doesn't concern me. What does concern me is how you see me. I wanted you to know the truth, and in divulging it to you, I've now put you at risk. I've put our families at risk, too."

"How so?" she demanded, turning her hand

over, taking his and holding it.

"If Cardona or one of his soldiers ever recognizes me, they'll hunt me down and kill me. And they won't stop there. They'll take out both of our families."

"But you said you were under an alias."

"Yes, and I also wore a beard to hide my face. But I can't ever be a hundred percent sure that someday, one of his soldiers might accidentally spot me."

"Do you think he's looking for you?"

"I don't know. I'm hoping he thinks I'm in a federal prison somewhere with a lot of his other drug soldiers. He has no way of tracking me down. In his business? Men die all the time and there's so many others to take that man's place. I wasn't important to Cardona. Chances are, he'll write me off like he will the rest of his men that got rounded up that night, and forget all of us. Out of sight, out of mind."

"He'll probably just chalk it up to experience, and move on, like you said."

Mark moved his finger across the back of her hand, holding her worried gaze. "I didn't want you thinking the worst of me, Mattie. I see-sawed over telling you why I suddenly left you again. I could see the damage it had done. I wanted, somehow, to repair it." He lifted his hand from hers, grazing her pale cheek. "You are so important to me, Mattie. I think you've always known that. But now I'm speaking up about it because I don't want to live my life without you in it. You're the most important person in the world to me."

His tone was almost pleading, but he didn't care. If he couldn't have Mattie, he'd have no reason for living. She was the light, the hope, in his life. His reason for being. His reason to fight every day to heal his inner wounds and become a better man.

"From the day we met, Mattie, as first graders, we were drawn to one another. You just naturally reached out those loving arms of yours and put them around me. We became friends and then, over time, we became inseparable."

She pressed against his opened palm that gently cradled her cheek. Closing her eyes, Mattie choked back tears. Then, she confirmed what he most wanted to hear. "We are still that way to this day, Mark."

"Are you sure?" he rasped, his hand tightening over hers.

"I'm very sure."

"But you were withholding from me, Mattie. I could feel it."

Nodding, she sighed and slid her other hand into his. "You're right. I felt shut out of your life, Mark, because you left without an explanation. Now I know why. And I agree you had to do this. Wyatt's up to his butt in the security industry, and I understand that you can't share what you do on assignment." Her voice rose, and she was overcome with emotion. "I'm so glad you told me, Mark. When you left at eighteen, I nearly died of heartbreak."

"I could see the wall it placed between us, Mattie." He traced each of her long, slender fingers. "And I didn't know how to remove that barrier between us. But since I've been back, I knew I had to tell you about the undercover work or I'd lose you forever. I could feel it coming."

"I just don't have the strength to lose you again, Mark."

"I got it, Mattie."

Her fingers closed over his. "Thank you for coming clean. It means the world to me."

Nodding, wanting to kiss her senseless, Mark knew he had to pace their relationship. Mattie would probably liken it to a split blanket being knitted back together again. One knit and purl at a time. "I knew it would."

"I just wish," she said, "that the townspeople knew what you've done. I hate the idea of you being the target of unjust gossip."

He shook his head. "My name in this town was muddied when I was born, Mattie. I've learned to live with it. The only person I want to know who I really am, is you. Only you . . ."

# CHAPTER 11

*February 14*

ANXIETY SHOT THROUGH Mark as he mounted the steps to Mattie's kindergarten building. It was four p.m. He knew her schedule: by three p.m., the parents had all picked up their children, and now Mattie was cleaning up the room and preparing for the following day.

Mark had taken off early from his work at the Rocking L, shaved, showered, and changed his clothes. This was all part of his campaign to woo her back into his arms by becoming someone she could count on, now and forever.

He pulled the door open and stepped inside. The classroom was quiet, but he could hear Mattie puttering around in the service area—which had a sink—just behind the classroom. He heard water running and quietly closed the door. Yes, there she was, scrubbing out a bunch of mason jars holding tempera paint. She had cleaned all the brushes and neatly laid them out to dry on the other side of the sink. He knew how much she wanted the children to explore their own, unique creativity. Poster board and tempera paint were out in the classroom at least two to three times a week. And she always had the children's paintings, once dried, hung around the room. It looked more like an art gallery to Mark but he silently applauded her desire to allow the children their natural creativity, too.

He smiled, loving how she looked today. Long, curly strands of red hair framed her temples, while the rest of it was piled up in a loose top knot, captured by a colorful, purple plastic comb.

Always dressed sensibly, today she wore what she called her "granny" dress. In the winter around here, it got good and cold and during this time of the year, when days were frosty, he'd seen her wear wool dresses that fell to her ankles. Draped across her shoulders and tied in an artful knot at her throat, was a bright-red scarf worn to set off the neutral gray of the dress. She wore a black leather belt around her waist, giving the shapeless granny dress some style and complementing her curved hips.

Mark had to admit it, he enjoyed just watching Mattie work efficiently, giving one-hundred percent of her focus to the job before her. She had twenty preschoolers and about half the Mason jars were cleaned and set upside down on a towel to air dry. The other ten jars were a panorama of rainbow colors waiting their turn to be washed clean.

He turned, looking above the whiteboard to see twenty paintings hung to dry. The paintings were all different, each beautiful in its own way.

Turning, his gaze settled on Mattie once more. She wore a bright green apron to keep the paint from splashing across the front of her dress. Her hands were long, fingers slender, and he admired her ability to multi-task—the woman was a dedicated worker.

For a moment, Mark wondered what his life might have been like if his mother had survived and he'd had someone to make him feel wanted, loved, and worthwhile. Because Mattie was that way with her kids. They absolutely adored her in large and small ways.

"Mark!"

He jerked out of his reverie, lifting his chin. Mattie turned, startled. She hadn't expected him. Good.

"Hey, I thought you might like some Valentine's Day flowers and candy." He moved forward, a dozen red roses in his right hand, and a huge, three-pound box of heart-shaped chocolates in the other one. Her eyes widened, her lips forming an 'O', delighting him that she was truly surprised.

"Oh, my goodness!" she whispered, quickly grabbing a nearby terrycloth towel and wiping her damp hands. "Mark! I never expected this!" She flew toward him with a huge smile of gratitude.

His grin deepened and he stopped, holding out the roses wrapped in pink tissue paper with a white ribbon around them. "Well, now maybe I can do things I've always dreamed of doing for you, but was never here to see them through." His voice became suddenly thick. "Now, I can. Here, these are for you. They're long overdue . . ."

Her face suddenly crumpled as her hands gently cupped the bouquet. She brought them to her nose, closing her eyes, inhaling.

Just watching her, Mark could barely resist taking her in his arms and kissing her soft lips. When Mattie opened her eyes, he asked, anxiously, "Are they all right? I know you like roses . . ."

"I love roses," she managed, her voice awash with feelings. Her fingers trembled as they touched the half-opened flowers.

"And here's the candy part of this occasion," he added, holding out the box to her. "I know you like Whitman Samplers, and I got lucky and found some."

Mattie's smile widened as she took the heavy, heart-shaped box. "I hope you're going to help me eat these, Reuss. This is a lot of candy!"

"Well," he said, "I thought that maybe your kids here at the kindergarten might like some."

"You're so sweet!" she cried. "That's so thoughtful of you!"

"I'm far from that, Mattie, but I'm glad you like the flowers and chocolates." He swallowed hard and rasped, "Happy Valentine's Day." And then, he opened up the black leather vest he wore over his light-blue, flannel long-sleeved shirt. "I almost forgot . . . here . . ." He handed her a thick, large white envelope.

"I'm . . . just . . . overwhelmed, Mark," Mattie gushed. "Come and sit down at the table while I put the roses in water. And then I'll open your wonderful card."

Pushing his damp palms down his jeans, he worried about what he'd written in the card. What would Mattie do? How would she react? Unsure, Mark followed her to the small round table and sat down, watching her put water in a vase for her beloved red roses.

She removed the apron, setting it to one side and dried her hands on a towel. Then, she took his card and slipped it into the pocket of her granny dress. Every once in a while, Mattie would stop, press her face into the blossoms and smell them. It made Mark feel as if he'd really pleased her. Yes, he could tell he had—she was beyond happy. And it was only a small measure of what he owed her after all these years of love and loyalty.

"You deserve flowers every day for the rest of your life," he told her.

Mattie tilted her head in his direction, lifting the vase out of the sink. "You know how much I love them. You see how many I've planted around my little house."

"It's one of the hundreds of good things about you, Mattie."

She gave him a warm look, walked over to where he sat, and placed the vase to one side of the small table.

He got up, pulling out the other chair for her.

"Thank you," she whispered, sitting down and taking his card from her pocket. Placing it in front of her, she nudged the chocolates in his direction. "Why don't you open these while I read your card?"

Mark would have preferred watching her expression as she read, but he did as she asked. It was a simple card, with a bouquet of wildflowers on the front of it, encircled by a glittering pink heart. Inside, the card was blank, allowing plenty of room for Mark to write a message to Mattie about how he truly felt. He had labored for almost two days, trying to find the right tone, the right words, to express his heart to Mattie without saying outright, I love you.

Those fragile, beautiful, forever words were reserved only for her. But he couldn't push or stress her with his goal of asking for her hand in marriage. All of that would have to wait. Mattie had to have time to adjust to Mark 2.0. Would she like what he said? His heart was racing with a mixture of fear and hope, but if he was honest with himself, it was mostly fear.

MATTIE COULD SEE the concern in Mark's gold-brown eyes. She saw him struggling to appear relaxed, but she could sense tension ramping up within him. Running her fingers across the embossed surface, giving him a look of gratitude, she said, "You know how I love flowers. This is perfect, Mark."

A bit of tension left the corners of his mouth, and he said, "I hope you like what I wrote inside it. I mean every word of it, Mattie."

She opened it, cradling the card. "I know I will . . ."

*Moonlight brings out the emerald green in your eyes, and I drown in the radiance that shines through them, embracing me. You heal my fractured soul.*

*Sunlight kisses your hair and a riot of gold, copper, and crimson, like a flame, becomes your halo telling me how much of angel you are in my dark life.*

*Your freckles remind me of the Milky Way covering the night sky with its ephemeral beauty. I celebrate who you really are, hiding nothing of your true self.*

*The smile you share with me has always calmed me, made my heart beat faster, made me feel whole even when I'm not.*

*Your voice is soft velvet and my ears hungrily listen and absorb your words, because your words are music to me.*

*When you laugh, it lifts me out of my darkness and makes me feel hope for a better life.*

*And when you touch me, I feel complete. I feel a wholeness I've never had before in my life.*

*I don't know how one person can be so much to another, but you are all of that to me and always will be. Forever.*

*Thank you for never giving up on me. Thank you for seeing me, not my wounds and scars that I will carry for the rest of my life. I'll always care about you, Mattie. And I will always be there for you. Mark.*

Mattie could barely pull in a breath, her eyes riveted on the scrawled ink words. The utter honesty of Mark unveiling himself to her tore through her, intensifying her love for him as never before. Lifting her lashes, she saw how awkward he felt, how worried he was that he was less than the man she wanted. She sensed he was trying to brace himself against her not liking what he'd written.

Slowly closing the card, she pressed it with both her hands against her heart. "I never knew you held such beautiful thoughts about me, Mark. I'm stunned, in a good way. Actually, I'm at a loss for words, really . . ." Choking, tears burning hotly in her eyes, she struggled to push them away, adding brokenly, "You really do see me."

"I always have, Mattie," he began, his voice buoyed by relief. "You do so much good for me."

She raised her hand, pushing the tears from her eyes with her fingers, giving him a tender look. "I'm going to cherish this card for the rest of my life. I'm putting it on my dresser where I can pick it up and read it on bad days when I'm feeling down. You have no idea how your words touch my heart, my soul, Mark. I just never knew you had this in you," she managed, giving him a wobbly, half smile of apology, searching his widening eyes.

He sat there, jaw moving, his eyes narrowed and intense upon her. "I'm not much of a writer . . ."

She managed a soft smile. "I love what you wrote to me, Mark! I love you for struggling so long to create the most beautiful card I've ever read." She moved her fingers in a caressing motion over the card and then placed it on the table in front of her. "I will cherish your words forever. I promise you that."

Shaking his head, he confessed, "You have no idea of how many times I wadded up the piece of paper I was writing on and threw it in the trash basket, only to start all over again. I needed to find exactly the right words that told you how I felt."

"How long did it take you to write this? It feels as if you really gave it your all."

"Honestly, I started it after we got back home from our lunch together at the stream."

"That was a wonderful day. I loved being with you, Mark. It was like a dream come true for me."

Cocking his head, he studied her. "What do you mean?"

Mattie shrugged, giving him an embarrassed look. "I used to dream, even as a teenager, of the things we'd do together. I thought about all the fun we'd have—the laughter and the good times. I remembered that whenever we could get away from your father, from your family ranch, you became a different, absolutely wonderful person."

"I kind of dreamed of things like that, too," he admitted, relaxing as she shared her joy with him.

"Really?"

A corner of his mouth lifted in amusement. "Yes, really."

Mattie was soaking up their conversation like a dry sponge. Times like this with Mark could be counted on one hand. Now, he was being raw, open, and brutally honest. Her heart glided upward, as if on an invisible rainbow of joy. She reached over, her hand curving over his fist on the table. Rubbing his hand gently, she felt him begin to relax.

"I'm still shaking from the beauty of your words on that card. I never knew you saw me like that, Mark. And it just makes me want to cry for utter joy because I feel so good about us."

He relaxed his fist, turned his hand over, carefully cradling hers. "I think I'm ready to leave my past behind. I want to write a new chapter in my own Book of Life, Mattie." His fingers curved around hers, his eyes never leaving her moist ones. "I want it to include you. What do you say?"

"That's easy. All my life," she said, "I've wanted just you, Mark. And now, just knowing what you told me about Juan and the DEA mission makes me confident that you really are home for good."

"I came home to you, Mattie, no one else."

"Well, I can tell you that I'm ready to write that new chapter with you. Although I must admit, I'm a little anxious."

"I'm scared to death, Mattie." His fingers caressed hers in light, stroking motions. "But I'm more afraid that I'll disappoint you someday, and that you'll walk away forever."

Giving a shake of her head, she said, "Never. The only thing that could tear us apart is for you to suddenly up and leave again. But I think we're past that, aren't we?"

His mouth pursed and he studied their clasped hands in the center of the table. "I'm home for good, Mattie. That's my promise to you."

She perked up, giving him a loving look. "Then what are we waiting for? Let's start writing that next chapter together!"

# CHAPTER 12

MATTIE COULDN'T HOLD back any longer. She pushed her chair back and saw Mark's questioning look as she quickly came around the table, placed her hands on his broad shoulders, and leaned down, pressing her mouth fully against his.

As she eased her lips along the seam of his, she felt his powerful reaction, his hands gripping her shoulders, holding her in place. With her eyes closed, she savored his opening mouth hungrily, just as starved as she was for him. Their breathing went from zero to sixty in a split second and she felt him trying to get a grip on himself, working through the shock that she was actually kissing him.

Tilting her head just a bit, she slid her lips across his, hearing him groan—a deep, rolling sound through his chest—and it spurred her on.

This was the sound of a man being pleasured and who wanted more. Her fingers dug deeper into his shoulders, his leather vest providing a delightful, nubby texture beneath her fingertips. He smelled of pure male: the lime soap he'd used before coming over here, the scent of saddle leather, and a hint of alfalfa hay. His hands ranged from her shoulders all the way down her back, sending sparks of heat as he stoked an inferno to life within her lower body.

She smiled against his mouth as he settled his hands around her waist, pushing the chair back, not wanting to lose contact with her, then guiding her to sit down across his lap.

Oh! This was so wonderful! The last time Mattie had kissed Mark was when they were in high school. Back then, they had exchanged tentative, innocent, searching kisses, and Mattie had never forgotten them. Mark's youthful desire had made her tremble with the need of something she had never felt, but wanted desperately to experience.

Now, she would—no more waiting for them! She lifted her hands to push her fingers lightly through his short, dark hair. Instantly, he growled with appreciation. Pushing him back into the chair, she wasn't about to end their first kiss as adults. No way!

She was starving for the taste, the smell, the hard body that belonged to Mark. She wanted these to belong to her, starting now.

Mark obviously felt the same way about her as his arms wrapped around her body, crushing her against his chest. Instantly, her nipples hardened and his slightest movements made her cry out from the pleasure he brought her.

Now, she gloried as she felt his long fingers stroking her spine, caressing her, letting her know he loved what they were sharing. Her desire to feel all of him broke open a dam of need that had been building for so long, she was swept away, rocketing wildly out of control.

Briefly, she pulled away from his mouth, staring deep into his golden eyes, now burning with need for her. Her breath came in gasps, she slid her hands across his hair, trailing them down his corded neck and finally cupping his jaw.

"Mark, I need you. I need you so badly I hurt. Don't tell me no. I want you to come home with me. I want to love you. I want you to love me." Her voice, shaken and needy, dropped to a whisper. "Please? Will you?"

His eyes narrowed, and suddenly, she knew how it felt to be hunted, a predator's delicious quarry. It wasn't frightening to her. How could it be? A throbbing blaze pulsed between her thighs in response to his look. She moaned softly as he cupped her hips, drawing her tightly against his erection.

"Are you sure?" he demanded harshly, his

hands becoming more firm on her hips. "Mattie?"

Gulping, she gave a jerky nod, unable to keep her fingers from moving across his tense shoulders, following the hard line of his jaw, starving to make him all hers. "I'm positive, Mark. I want you."

Their passion was interrupted by a soft, tender look from Mark as he swept his hands up over her shoulders, holding her more gently, cradling her precious body.

"I never thought I'd hear you say those words, Mattie. I honestly didn't."

She sat up a little, on fire now, her skin riffling wildly beneath any stroke or light, grazing movement of his fingers anywhere upon her. "You heard right, Reuss. Now let's get out of here before I take you down on this floor."

He shot her a grin, then slid his fingers along her temple, pushing those curly strands aside.

"Okay . . . yes, let's go to your house. Do you want to meet me there?"

"I don't want us to be separated for even a few minutes," she admitted breathlessly, unwilling to move just yet. "I've waited so long for this, Mark."

"So have I, sweet woman." He slid his hand around her nape, giving her a light kiss filled with promises to come. Pulling away, he said thickly, "Can you drive your truck home, Mattie? You're looking a little dazed."

She managed a squeak of a laugh, following the line of his broad shoulders as she sat upright on his lap. "I'm not sure. I feel all quivery inside, Mark. My knees feel weak and I'm not even standing up. I'm aching for you . . ."

Nodding, he said, "Let's walk over to my truck, Mattie, and I'll drive us to your house. Later, we'll pick up your truck here at the school."

She gave a nod. "Yes . . ."

"Let's get some things out of the way before we leave. I don't have any condoms on me. I never thought . . . well . . ."

"I've just finished my period, so I'm in a safe zone. I don't want to use a condom unless there's a reason. Is there?"

"I'm clean."

"So am I. So we're set. All I have to do is stand up and not collapse!" She gave a shy, girlish laugh.

"I'll keep a hold on your arm, sweetheart. Don't worry, I won't let you fall," he assured her.

Mattie knew Mark would take care of her. He always had, all his life. "Okay, here we go." She slid off his lap, feeling his hand wrap around her upper arm to steady her as she got to her feet. Laughing a little giddily, Mattie looked down at her legs. "I've never felt my knees go mushy!"

He unwound like a lithe cougar coming silently to his feet, and slid his arm around her shoulders. "I'm none too steady myself, Mattie. You're right, this has been a long time coming. Let's get your coat and purse."

She managed to make a sound of disbelief as they walked over to her dark-gray wool coat. "I can't even think straight. My brain is in park."

Chuckling a little, Mark kept one hand on Mattie's arm and lifted the coat off the hook. "Yeah, you look a little blown, but on you it looks beautiful. Let's get you into this coat."

MARK FELT AS if he were in one of his torrid dreams as he eased the dress off Mattie's head and shoulders, allowing her to pull her arms out of the sleeves. The wool felt wiry between his hands. He couldn't take his eyes off her. Mattie had a lush body, her hips provocatively flared, ending in those long, long legs of hers. She was a rancher's daughter and was far more fit than most women because of her years of hard, physical work.

She had sculpted creamy flesh that looked like perfection to him. She took the dress, walking across the shining, pecan-wood floor, and draped it over the back of a chair near her dresser. When she turned, he was blown away by the shape of her breasts, captured in a lacy black bra. The sight of her in it made his whole body harden.

When he saw her tiny, lace bikini panties, his erection throbbed. Mattie reminded him of the women painted by the old masters of Europe: lush, full-breasted, their curves and softness accentuated.

"You," he breathed, as she walked slowly toward him, "are incredibly beautiful." He saw her smile, that glint in her darkening green eyes, the way she walked, that womanly sway of her hips as she approached him. Could he really be living out one of his torrid dreams about her? If so, he didn't want to awaken. Not this time.

Reaching out, Mattie eased her fingers beneath his leather vest, spreading her fingers across his chest to slide the vest off his shoulders.

"And you look so incredibly handsome, strong, and sexy to me," she whispered near his ear as she began to unbutton his blue flannel shirt. Her fingers were trembling—but so were his.

Streaks of pleasure coursed through his arms and chest as she opened his shirt and helped him out of it. Beneath it, he wore a white t-shirt. His breath caught as she slid her palms across his chest. He saw the satisfaction and desire on her face, her skin flushed, her eyes dazed with pleasure.

"I can't handle a slow undress," he rasped,

moving away from her.

She laughed breathily, watching him sit down on the edge of the bed, haul off his cowboy boots and black socks, and toss them aside. Standing, he quickly opened his belt buckle, unzipped, and removed his jeans.

She gazed at him now, his erection getting all her attention. Her eyes crinkled and her smile deepened, liking what she saw. A decade of life had separated them and she was no longer the young, inexperienced girl he once knew—but he wasn't either.

"You are more than just sexy," she said huskily.

"Likewise," he growled, walking up to her, sliding his hands around her and unhooking her bra. "Your turn, sweet woman."

Mattie gasped as he removed the black bra revealing her full breasts. It made him want to drag her off to the bed right now—but he also wanted to enjoy the wonder of savoring this moment.

"We've waited a long time for this," he told her, sliding his thumbs beneath the elastic of her panties, slowly crouching in front of her and drawing them downward. Mattie placed her hand on his shoulder to balance herself as she lifted one foot and then the other.

Mark gave her an appreciative gaze from head to toe, placing his hands on her shoulders as she stood proudly before him, naked. To his surprise, she was proud and confident—not self-conscious, and he loved her even more for that. Mattie was a strong woman in so many ways but he was going to have her, and she was going to be all his.

She locked her gaze with his, sliding her hands up across his chest, her fingers tangling in the soft, dark strands of hair spread across it. "You're right, we have waited a long time," she whispered unsteadily. "I feel as if I'm in one of my erotic dreams."

His mouth pulled upward. "You too, huh? Did you dream of me, Mattie?" He glided his fingers in a stroking motion across her shoulders, watching her nipples pucker and grow hard, begging to be touched and suckled.

Laughing lightly, she said, "Oh, if you only knew how many dreams I've had just like we are now in this moment!"

He joined her laughter, sliding his hands down the length of her arms, capturing one of her hands. "I think we can probably compare and the number of times would pretty much match, don't you think?" He tugged at her hand, leading her toward the bed.

"You're right," she admitted, coming to a halt and standing before him.

Mark wasn't surprised when she placed her hands on his shoulders, pushing and guiding him down on the mattress. He liked her assertiveness because it suited her—Texas women weren't shy! He lay on his back, watching her join him, coming to rest on her knees, and leaning over him. "Touch me all you want," he invited, his voice guttural. He saw a feral look come to her eyes, appreciating her as never before.

"Oh, I'm going to touch you everywhere, Mark Reuss. I've waited too long and I'm going to love you completely, so I hope you're ready . . ."

Her husky words, thick with emotion, flowed through him. He reached up, gently removing the comb from her hair, watching it tumble like a living flame down across her shoulders as she leaned down, kissing the column of his neck, trailing her wet, soft lips down across his shoulder, to his chest. Her hands were busy, gliding, seeking, caressing, and he groaned.

"Mattie . . . I can't handle much more . . ."

She eased her leg across his narrow hips. "I can't either," she said, breathless, "I need you, Mark . . ."

His whole world turned into a blazing furnace of need as she slid her wet core against his thick erection. It was the most profound sensation she had ever felt—a meeting, a coming together, a celebration of so many years apart, and now, they were here, together at last.

He gritted his teeth as she eased downward,

drawing him into her heated, tight body. He gripped her hips, beginning to move, thrusting his hips upward slowly, giving her body time to accommodate him. Mark met and matched the rhythm she was establishing for them. Little, happy sounds emanated from her throat. Her head was lifted, eyes tightly shut, lips parted, her fingers digging into his chest.

It took every bit of control for Mark not to explode on the spot, but to give Mattie a chance to luxuriate in the same silky sensations clasping him, sliding around him. Clenching his teeth, jaw rigid, he brought Mattie into firm contact with him. He heard her gasp, a little cry of surprise, suddenly tensing. Yes! More than anything, Mark wanted to give her an orgasm, bring her along and pleasure her as much as she wanted to pleasure him.

Suddenly, Mattie felt her whole upper body jerk backward, and she threw her head back with a feral cry. She felt her body clench around his erection, and then luxuriated in the flood of moisture surrounding his member. Mark kept up the rhythm, pulling her back and forth upon him, increasing the intensity of her release.

Never had he felt as joyous as he did now, sharing his body and soul with Mattie. Just as she began to emerge from the rapture of a climax, he allowed himself to release deeply within her. There was such a powerful sensation of fulfillment, of connection, and of being one with her, that all he could do was growl her name in gratitude.

The heat rolled down his spine, slamming through him and flooding into her receptive, welcoming body. Swimming through a hazy dream-like world, all he could see were lights exploding behind his closed eyelids. His whole body shimmered with heat, with relief, with a soaring happiness that overwhelmed all his senses.

Mark heard Mattie call his name as she sank down upon his torso, resting her brow against his jaw, her arms sliding beneath his neck, holding him, loving him. And nothing had ever felt so good as right now in the aftermath of their coupling.

He moved his face into her fragrant hair, inhaling, feeling her softness and at the same time, her womanly strength as she wrapped herself around him, body and soul.

Tears leaked from the corners of his tightly shut eyes as he slid his arms across her back, crushing her against him fully, hearing musical sounds in the back of her throat as she nestled against his neck. This moment would indelibly be branded into his thundering heart, his memory, and his essence for the rest of his life.

"I love you, Mattie. I've always loved you . . ." He choked, fighting back the tears, holding her as tightly as he could.

Mattie sobbed, pressing her face against his neck, her arms tightening around his shoulders. "And I love you so much, Mark . . . so much . . . oh, God, and for so long . . . so long."

Her broken words were filled with anguish, and relief flowed through them both. Now, he was inside her, where he belonged. She was a vessel of love in every possible way, and Mark was lost in a landscape of endless beauty floating past his closed eyelids. Mattie was so warm, her flesh velvety against his sweaty skin. She was all curves to his linear body. Time didn't exist—only Mattie existed.

There was nothing more Mark would ever need or want in his life except the woman he now held in his arms. She lay like a warm, wonderful blanket over his body. Her breasts pressed into his chest, their hips joined, his arms holding her and never wanting to let her go.

Opening his hand, he skimmed her back, caressing her. He loved the mewing sound of pleasure vibrating within her over his touch, his adoration. Pressing a soft kiss against her temple, he rasped, "I love you Mattie. I'll never stop loving you. You're mine and I'm yours for as long as you want me—hopefully, forever."

# CHAPTER 13

MATTIE SLOWLY OPENED her eyes. The clock on the bed stand read five a.m. She had never felt as wonderful as she did right now. Mark lay spooned around her, one arm beneath her neck, his other arm draped across her waist. She felt as if she was now, finally, his—deeply desired and perfectly loved.

She closed her eyes again, absorbing the feeling of Mark behind her, wrapped against her backside. She felt his slow, moist breath against the nape of her neck, her flesh tingling.

Mattie was, for the first time in her life, utterly satisfied. How she loved this man! Despite the depth of his wounds, Mark still had so much goodness in him. He fought daily to break free of the mental and emotional prison that Jeb had placed him in. She was so proud of him, loving him even more, if that was possible, for his personal courage. He would not allow his toxic past to taint what they had now with one another.

Mark groaned and mumbled something into her hair. Then, Mattie felt him press his hard, lean body against hers, his arm tightening momentarily around her, drawing her closer to him. As if he couldn't live without her. She felt his lips nudging her nape, kissing her—she'd never been so deliriously happy.

Slowly, she extricated herself, turned over, and faced him. His eyes were barely open, filled with drowsiness, and perhaps, for the first time, she saw Mark without any defenses in place.

The relaxation in his face was remarkable, making him seem even more handsome than he already was in her eyes. She smiled and whispered, "I want to wake up every morning just like this with you." Mattie threaded her fingers through a few strands of black hair, easing them off his unlined brow.

Mark lifted his hand, catching hers, guiding it between them. He pushed upward on his other elbow, leaning down, capturing her lips, a lingering, love-filled kiss shared between them. Drawing inches away, he looked deep into her eyes. "We will," he said, his voice deep with promise.

Sighing, she caressed his stubbly jaw, her hand resting at the crook between his neck and shoulder. "There's so much we need to talk about, but I have to get ready for school."

"I know. And your dad is expecting me at eight this morning to help him move a bull to another pasture."

She smiled up at him, caressing his cheek. "There will be time at night when we get back from work . . . and weekends."

Nodding, Mark said, "I want to live with you, Mattie. And if you want the same thing, and I think you do, we need to let your family know."

"Yes . . . maybe at Sunday dinner when we all get together. We could invite Sage over, too. Would you like that?"

"I would. I think she'll be very happy to hear our news. Until then, we've got evenings to talk about details."

She eased out of his arms and sat up, her hair tumbling forward across her shoulders. "Yes . . . the details . . . but the important thing is we're together now."

"WE HAVE AN announcement to make," Mattie told her family on Sunday afternoon as everyone assembled around the dinner table, eagerly anticipating a wedge of cherry pie alongside two scoops of vanilla ice cream for dessert. They had just finished eating and everything had been cleared from the table. Sage was pouring fresh coffee for everyone. She had brought two homemade cherry pies over to the ranch for dessert and they were sitting on the table along with a tub of ice cream.

Mattie felt a warm glow as she gave Mark, who sat at her left, a quick smile. He responded with a look filled with love. Earlier at her home, they had made love once again, and that after-glow still resonated strongly within her belly, the pleasure continuing to throb within her.

"Oh?" Daisy said, her gray brows rising. "About what, Mattie?"

Mattie managed a nervous smile, but Mark placed his hand over hers, giving her the courage she needed. "Mark and I are together." She cast a quick glance over at her siblings, Jake and Cat, and Sage, who sat on the opposite side of the table from them, to see their reaction. She saw surprise and then wide smiles. "And . . . we love one another. We want to live together and see how it goes."

Hank nodded, giving his wife at the other end of the table an "I-told-you-so" look. His gaze shifted to Mark.

"Welcome to the family, son. Daisy and I are more than happy to hear this is happening."

Mattie grinned happily, squeezing Mark's rough, calloused hand. He winked at her. "Then you're all okay with it?"

Daisy chuckled. "Honey, you were probably

the only one at this table who didn't expect this to happen. Of course we're happy for both of you."

Jake grinned at Mark. "I was wondering why you showed up late the last few mornings."

Snorting, Mark said, "It's tough leaving your sister."

"You're so romantic," Mattie sighed, leaning over, giving him a kiss on his cheek.

"So?" Hank rumbled, cutting into the cherry pie, "What have you kids decided?"

"Well," Mattie began coyly, "marriage and then we want to start a family as soon as possible, Dad." She touched her belly beneath the purple, wool sweater dress she wore.

Daisy clapped her hands. "Hallelujah! We'll finally have a grandchild, Hank!"

Hank raised a brow. "That's gonna be right nice, Daisy."

"Well," Mattie gushed, "if it happens, it happens. Mark and I just want to let things unfold naturally. If I don't get pregnant right away, we're okay with that, too."

"Looks like Pepe's house is going to be empty again," Hank noted wryly.

"I'll still be your wrangler," Mark said, becoming serious once more. "Nothing changes unless you want it to, Hank."

Shrugging his broad shoulders, Hank spooned some ice cream into his mouth. After swallowing, he said, "Son, what changes is that as part of our family, officially, you are going to be in training to be one of my foremen. And someday, you'll be sharing those duties with Jake, who is already trained as a foreman, once me and Daisy are too old to handle the place anymore." He gave Jake and Mark a proud look. "And both of you are good wranglers—smart, responsible, and I know the Rocking L will be in the best of hands between you two."

"I'm looking forward to it, Dad," Jake said, giving Mark a happy grin.

"Mattie, if you get pregnant are you going to keep teaching?" Daisy asked.

"Oh, for sure," she said.

"She'll always be a teacher," Mark murmured encouragingly. "And we intend to live in Mattie's home at the edge of Van Horn for now."

"But," Hank interjected, "we could get busy with construction plans to enlarge Pepe's house for you and your coming family. How about three new bedrooms as additions? If we do that, would you and Mattie like to live with us on the spread? Would the house be large enough? It's only eight miles to Van Horn, Mattie, and you could drive to and from here without a problem."

"Oh, I hadn't even thought about that yet, Dad." She looked at Mark. "How do you feel about living here?"

"I'm fine with it as long as you're happy."

"Well," she admitted, "my house is small, and honestly, I was worried that if I got pregnant we'd have to move, Mark."

"Then," Hank said in his best Texas drawl, "it's all settled. You two stay there until we can hire a construction company to come out and make that little ranch house what you and Mark want, Mattie. We'd be much happier if you were out here, with us."

"Yes," Daisy said, "especially for a first pregnancy. I wouldn't worry so much because we're near if you needed any assistance."

Mattie gave all of them a grateful look. "This is such a wonderful solution, thank you."

"Mark doesn't care where he lives as long as he's with Mattie," Sage added in an amused tone, giving her brother a warm look of congratulations.

"You're right," Mark agreed.

"So many happy changes," Cat joined in, giving her older sister a pleased glance.

Mattie dragged in a deep breath. Mark seemed calm compared to her own growing excitement, and knowing how deeply he loved her was all she'd ever need.

"It wasn't like these changes happened overnight," Hank said.

"No," Mark admitted, "they didn't." He traded a look with Mattie. "But your daughter's heart is large and patient. She waited for me until

I finally came home to stay."

"You two," Daisy said, a catch in her voice, wiping tears from her eyes, "have always been meant for one another."

"But secrets had to be unveiled and revealed," Mattie whispered, holding her mother's soft gaze. "Secrets that Mark and I withheld from one another, fearing if we ever spoke of our hidden love for each other it might scare the other person off."

"Or," Mark said, "that the other person would say no."

"Secrets can tear a family apart," Daisy agreed, giving them both a look of understanding.

Sage said, "Mark, will you ever tell us why you left suddenly for four months?"

Shaking his head, he said, "No. Never." He released Mattie's hand and slid his arm around her shoulders in a comforting gesture. "It's a secret that will go to the grave with me. It's one that never needs to be spoken about again."

"From now on," Mattie whispered, giving Mark a loving glance, "there will be no more secrets between us."

Sage nodded, thoughtfully. "I'm over the moon for both of you. It's time Mark received some happiness. No one deserves it more than he does."

"Thanks," Mattie told her. "It's a dream

come true for both of us."

MARK SAT ON the couch with Mattie in his arms as they watched the news later that night at her home. The clock read ten p.m. and she was snuggled beneath his left arm, leaning against him, her knees drawn up, resting against his thigh. Most of all, he liked that her lavender flannel gown fell to her ankles.

With Mattie's cheek against his shoulder, he'd never felt more fulfilled. He really hadn't known what happiness was until now. Mattie had always given him joy, but to love her, fill her with himself, hold her, and hear those sweet cries of pleasure were beginning to heal his heart and soul.

Finally, he belonged to someone. And she belonged to him. Closing his eyes, resting his head against hers, he felt years of torment drain out of him. It almost felt like a physical release, it was that intense. His childhood traumas were being dissolved by the richness of Mattie loving him in so many ways. It was as if he were sloughing off an old skin, getting rid of it one day at a time. Living with Mattie was breathing new life, and new hope, into him.

They had talked early Friday morning after making hungry love with one another about her possibly getting pregnant. Mattie had been wary, afraid he wouldn't want children. But when she heard he did want them so he could give them all the love he'd never received from his own father, she felt bring children into the world would be deeply healing for him.

Mattie had cried then and he'd cried with her. He hadn't cried since he was ten years old, but encircled in Mattie's arms, he let go and surrendered over to a higher power called love. And since then, he'd felt cleansed, lighter and happier than he thought he ever deserved to be. Their intimacy with one another only deepened and broadened as a result of giving one another the ultimate trust: their tears and pain.

The future ahead of them looked bright with so many good things about to happen. Next week, he'd take Mattie into the Van Horn jewelry store. Mark was an old-fashioned Texan by birth and believed in marriage, not just living together.

He wanted to watch her choose a set of rings she really loved, and then they would become officially engaged. He was proud of his woman. Not only was Mattie his life partner, she was his best friend, and the love of his life. And nothing in the world would ever change that!

## THE BEGINNING…

Don't miss Lindsay McKenna's next DELOS
series novella,

**Never Enough**

Available from Lindsay McKenna and Blue
Turtle Publishing and wherever you buy eBooks!

Turn the page for a sneak peek.

# Excerpt from

## Novella: Never Enough, Book 3B1
## Sequel to Forged in Fire, Book 3

THE AQUAMARINE OCEAN water was warm and delicious feeling over Dara's bare feet. Her sandals hung from the fingers of Matt's left hand. The sea breeze infused her with a peaceful feeling, as did the cries of seagulls sailing overhead. Walking on a golden, sandy beach, ankle-deep in the ocean water, made her feel so alive. Matt had taken off his sandals as well. The noontime warmth of the sun fell over her; the temperature was perfect, in the high seventies. The early January weather in Hawaii was very different from the climate she'd left back home in Virginia!

Every once in awhile, Dara would spot a small shell in the clear ocean water and she would stop, lean over, and retrieve her new treasure. Matt knew that locals here would get up at dawn, come down, and scour the beach for shells that had washed up during the night hours. By noon, the beaches were cleaned of any beautiful, whole

shells that had been deposited. But Dara delighted in the pieces of colorful shells that she found,
holding them like treasures in her hand. His heart
swelled with love for her; she was one of those
people who delighted in whatever she was doing.

He stopped her and said, "Why don't you
put your shells in the pocket of your dress?"

Laughing, she opened her palm, showing him
the shards. "They're so beautiful I just want to
hold them for a while. Even though they're
fractured and in pieces, I want to collect a bunch
of them while we're here. I've decided to put
them in a small glass goblet with the sand I'm
walking on. Next time we come down here, I'll
bring some plastic bags. I want to bring some of
Hawaii home with us where I can see it every
day."

"So," he said, moving his finger through her
many shell pieces, "you're going to put that glass
somewhere you can see it to remember this
time?" He melted beneath the joy he saw shining
in her eyes, those lips so lush, so kissable, and he
ached to do just that.

Dara smiled and nodded. "I'm putting this
on the desk in my office at the hospital. On
tough days, I can sit there and look at it and
remember this time with you."

Leaning over, he caressed her smiling mouth
with his. Matt could taste the salt air on her lips,
taste the mocha latte she'd had earlier before they

walked down to the beach. Easing away, he rasped, "I'm taking a heart photo of you right now . . ." He brought her gently to a stop, easing her into his body, feeling her breasts pressing into his chest, that low, husky sound of pleasure vibrating in her throat as he kissed her long and well. She was such a sensual, sexual creature, although most would never see it. He sure had when she belly danced at Bagram. And he'd been privileged to go with her to the gym where she worked out and belly danced to stay in top shape. They always ended up in bed after that, each of them turned on by the other.

Dara closed her eyes, drowning in Matt's cherishing mouth, his arm around her, bringing her into the fold of his tall, lean, hard body. Everything was perfect. Just perfect.

# The Books of Delos

Title: ***Last Chance*** (Prologue)
Publish Date: July 15, 2015
Learn more at:
delos.lindsaymckenna.com/last-chance

Title: ***Nowhere to Hide***
Publish Date: October 13, 2015
Learn more at:
delos.lindsaymckenna.com/nowhere-to-hide

Title: ***Tangled Pursuit***
Publish Date: November 11, 2015
Learn more at:
delos.lindsaymckenna.com/tangled-pursuit

Title: ***Forged in Fire***
Publish Date: December 3, 2015
Learn more at:
delos.lindsaymckenna.com/forged-in-fire

Title: ***Broken Dreams***
Publish Date: January 2, 2016
Learn more at:
delos.lindsaymckenna.com/broken-dreams

Title: ***Blind Sided***
Publish Date: June 5, 2016
Learn more at:
delos.lindsaymckenna.com/blind-sided

Title: ***Secret Dream***
Publish Date: July 25, 2016
Learn more at:
delos.lindsaymckenna.com/secret-dream

Title: ***Hold On***
Publish Date: August 3, 2016
Learn more at:
delos.lindsaymckenna.com/hold-on

Title: **Hold Me**
Publish Date: August 11, 2016
Learn more at
delos.lindsaymckenna.com/hold-me

Title: **Unbound Pursuit**
Publish Date: September 29, 2016
Learn more at:
delos.lindsaymckenna.com/unbound-pursuit

# Everything Delos!

## Newsletter

Please sign up for my free quarterly newsletter on the front page of my official Lindsay McKenna website at lindsaymckenna.com. The newsletter will have exclusive information about my books, publishing schedule, giveaways, exclusive cover peeks, and more.

## Delos Series Website

Be sure to drop by the website dedicated to the Delos series at delos.lindsaymckenna.com. There will be new articles on characters, publishing schedule and information about each book written by Lindsay.

## Quote Books

I love how the Internet has evolved. I had great fun create "quote books with text" which reminded me of an old fashioned comic book . . . lots of great color photos and a little text, which forms a "book" that tells you, the reader, a story. Let me know if you like these quote books because I think it's a great way to add extra enjoyment with this series! Just go to my Delos Series website delos.lindsaymckenna.com, which features the books in the series.

The individual downloadable quote books are located on the corresponding book pages. Please share with your reader friends!

42668608R00120

Made in the USA
Middletown, DE
19 April 2017